D0050657

The Reinvention of Edison Thomas

The Reinvention of Edison Thomas

JACQUELINE HOUTMAN

Front Street
Honesdale, Pennsylvania

CIP data is available.

FRONT STREET
An Imprint of Boyds Mills Press, Inc.
815 Church Street
Honesdale, Pennsylvania 18431

CONTENTS

The Reinvention of Edison Thomas

1. The Science Un-Fair

Eddy sat on the steps outside Drayton Middle School, where the noise from the science fair in the gym still roared in his head. Tiffany always told him to picture a calm place when he felt stressed. He thought of the rocky beach. He tried to remember the rhythmic lapping sound of the waves and the feel of the rocks pushing up against the soles of his feet. He inhaled deeply. The smell of the cool evening breeze told him rain was on the way.

He put two fingers up to the side of his throat and felt the pulsing of his carotid artery, the blood vessel that delivers blood to the brain. Tiffany's strategy wasn't working; his heart was still beating too fast. His body would have to be under control for him to go back into that gym full of people.

New Calming Strategy: think about the science fair project. He had wrapped copper wire from an old washing machine motor around an iron pipe. It seemed so simple, but when he ran an electric current through it, the opposing magnetic fields sent a copper ring flying nearly up to the rafters of the gym. That must have impressed the judges. Eddy would win first place for sure.

He was calmer now. He felt for the artery again and

looked at his watch. This was the best watch he'd ever had. Like most modern watches, it used the vibrations of a quartz crystal, instead of springs and gears, to tell time accurately. Eddy's watch was accurate to within one second every ten years. It also had a stopwatch that was accurate to hundredths of seconds. It had an alarm. It could tell him the time in four different time zones. It was water resistant to one hundred meters.

A drop of rain splashed directly onto the face of his watch. Another fell on his head. A raindrop landed on his right knee, leaving a dark circle on the faded denim of his jeans.

Eddy realized that he still had his finger on his neck but he hadn't started timing yet. He waited until his watch read 7:34:00 p.m. and started counting pulsations. When his watch read 7:34:15 p.m., he had counted to twenty-two. Twenty-two times four is eighty-eight. Eighty-eight beats per minute was still a little fast, but it would have to do. The rain fell more insistently. He took another deep breath, stood up, and walked into the school as raindrops filled in the dry spot on the concrete step where Eddy had been sitting.

Fact Number 212 from the Random Access Memory of Edison Thomas: Petrichor, the distinctive smell of rain on dry ground, is caused by plant oils released into the air from clay-based rocks and soil.

As he stepped through the doors to the gym, the noise closed in on him, surrounding him on all sides. The pounding of rain on the metal roof added an extra dimension of sound bombardment. He locked his eyes on his eddy coil display and wove his way through the crowd toward it. His dad was leaning over a nearby exhibit, examining the various spoiled foods so closely that he touched the plastic cover of the display with the brim of his Drayton Electrical Supply baseball cap.

"Look at this mold," said Dad. "It's pink. I never saw pink mold before."

Eddy looked at it. "It could be fungal, but it is more likely to be bacterial growth."

"I assume you're feeling better," said Dad.

"A little," said Eddy. It helped to concentrate on the exhibits. Some were very cool, like the wind tunnel for testing airplane designs. The poster behind it displayed the drag coefficients for planes—from the Wright brothers' biplane to modern military jets.

Other projects were unimpressive, like one exhibit with shoeboxes representing different ecosystems—the desert, the rain forest, the pond. The plastic animals in the ecosystems were not all to the same scale; in the African savanna box, the lions (*Panthera leo*, thought Eddy) were twice as big as the elephants (*Loxodonta africana*). A completely white box contained a polar bear (*Ursus maritimus*), two harbor seals (*Phoca vitulina*), a tiny little walrus (*Odobenus rosmarus*), and some emperor penguins (*Aptenodytes forsteri*).

"Those mammals live in the Arctic, but *Aptenodytes forsteri* lives only in Antarctica," Eddy pointed out a little too loudly. "In fact, there are no penguins at all that are native to the Northern Hemisphere."

"Keep your voice down, Eddy," whispered his dad. "There are seals in Antarctica, aren't there?"

"There are six kinds of seals in the Antarctic, but the harbor seal is not one of them," said Eddy in a deeper voice.

"That brain of yours is just full of useless facts, isn't it," sighed Dad.

"RAM, Dad," stated Eddy. "Random access memory."

"*Random* is a good word for it," said Dad.

"Anyway, emperor penguins can not be in the same ecosystem as harbor seals, walruses, and polar bears," continued Eddy. "How stupid can you be?"

"I think these are pretty good," said Dad. "It looks like a lot of work went into them."

"They could at least get the animals right," insisted Eddy. He scanned the room. He wanted to see Mitch's project. Mitch had spent a lot of time working on it, but he wouldn't tell Eddy what it was. "I am going to walk around for a while," Eddy told his dad.

An insistent tap on his back made Eddy turn around. He looked down at a sandstone-colored clump of hair sticking straight up from the top of a head. Eddy could see why they call that a cowlick. He pictured a cow licking the dull brown hair every morning before school.

"I like your project, Eddy," said the boy under the hair. The frames of his glasses were exactly the same color as his hair. "What would happen if you used direct current instead of alternating current?"

Eddy didn't say anything. He kept looking for Mitch.

"Did you see mine?" asked the boy eagerly. "The tornado chamber?"

Eddy caught sight of Mitch, which wasn't hard. Mitch Cooper was the tallest kid in school. Mitch was showing something on his cell phone to Will Pease.

"Hey, Mitch," yelled Eddy, walking quickly toward Mitch and Will, bumping into a few people along the way.

Mitch pocketed the cell phone and turned his face toward Eddy. "No need to shout, Professor. We can all hear you," he said. "So did you invent a machine to do my homework for me?"

"No," replied Eddy. "My project is about eddy coils."

"That was pretty conceited to name the thing after yourself."

"I did not name it after myself. It is named for the eddies of electrical current caused by the interaction between—"

"Yeah, right," said Mitch as he turned back to Will and laughed.

"I can not find your project," said Eddy.

Mitch grabbed Eddy by the shoulders and turned him 180 degrees. Eddy's body stiffened. He didn't usually like people getting that close to him, but he didn't want to say anything to his old friend Mitch. Mitch and Eddy had been friends for so long that Mitch should know that Eddy didn't like people getting that close.

"It's right over there," whispered Mitch in Eddy's ear, pointing over Eddy's shoulder at an exhibit between a forest of sweet potatoes (*Ipomoea batatas*) and a stroboscope. Eddy stepped toward the exhibit and away from Mitch, escaping the hot breath on his neck. Will whispered something to Mitch and they both laughed.

At the center of Mitch's exhibit, a laptop computer displayed a repeating loop of a shoot-em-up video game. No surprise there. Mitch liked video games. A lot. Big letters at the top of the poster board behind it read THE EFFECTS OF REPETITION ON EYE-HAND COORDINATION. A graph was taped to the poster board. The vertical axis was labeled "Maximum Game Level," and the horizontal axis was labeled "Number of Repetitions." Three crooked lines angled up across the graph.

Eddy pondered the graph for a moment. He supposed it meant that the more you play a game, the better you get at it. That seemed pretty obvious. The red and green lines were labeled *Will* and *Mark*. The blue line, Mitch's line, was above the other two, apparently indicating that Mitch was better than Will and Mark at this particular game—probably because Mitch owned the game and he had a chance to practice before the experiment started, reasoned Eddy.

A loud popping sound made Eddy jump. Mr. Benton, the principal, had turned on a microphone.

"Welcome," said Mr. Benton. "Welcome to the Twelfth Annual Drayton Middle School Science F..." His voice trailed off and he tapped on the microphone. "Terry, I don't think this is working," he shouted across the stage.

To the left of the stage, a kid with blue hair fiddled with some knobs on a console. Suddenly, the loudspeakers screamed, the sound stabbing into Eddy's brain. Eddy clamped his hands over his ears and squatted on the floor right where he stood. He stared down at the floor and rocked a little, looking at the floorboards, silently listing the elements in the periodic table.

He felt a hand on his shoulder, looked down at a pair of worn leather work boots, then up at his father. "You're fine," said his dad. "It's just a little feedback from the audio system."

"I know," said Eddy through clenched teeth. ... *chlorine, argon, potassium ...*

"Get up," said Dad. "People are watching you."

Eddy grunted and stared at the floor again. ... *scandium, titanium, vanadium ...*

By the time Eddy slowed his heart down, Mr. Benton had finished thanking everybody—the teachers, the parents, the judges, the sponsors, various elected officials, and even the custodians.

The sound of applause pushed on Eddy's brain. ... *manganese, iron, cobalt ...*

"And now, without further ado, the awards," said Mr. Benton. "Remember, folks, the top two finishers will go to the regional competition. The third-place finisher will be the alternate and will attend the regionals if, for any reason, the first- or second-place finisher is unable to attend.

Ms. Copeland, may I have the decision of the judges, please."

The science teacher walked up to the stage and handed Mr. Benton an envelope. Mr. Benton cleared his throat as he opened the envelope.

"For his project entitled 'Eddy Coil,' third place goes to Eddy Thomas." More applause, but not as loud this time.

Startled, Eddy looked up. THIRD? How was it possible that he had not won?

"Go on. Go get your ribbon," said Dad. "Take one of your deep breaths. You can do it."

Eddy looked up tentatively at his father, who was holding out a hand. "Go on," repeated his father.

Eddy grabbed the calloused hand and pulled himself up to standing. He turned his back to his dad and shuffled anxiously through the crowd, trying to ignore the noise, focusing his attention on the steps up to the stage.

Mitch walked up to Eddy from out of the crowd. "Good job," he said, patting Eddy on the back. Eddy smiled. Then he stumbled, but he regained his balance so he didn't fall.

Eddy walked up onto the stage, looking down at the steps so he wouldn't trip. A few people in the audience laughed, but he didn't understand why. He hadn't tripped. Mr. Benton handed him a white ribbon and said, "Congratulations, Eddy. You did a great job." Mr. Benton held his hand out to shake Eddy's hand, but Eddy continued looking at the floor and got off the stage as quickly as he could.

He found a relatively quiet place to gather his thoughts

behind a model of the Golden Gate Bridge. Third. How could Eddy's project only get third? The eddy coil was the best project at the science fair. It began raining harder, and the noise level in the gym increased.

He stroked the smooth satin ribbon.

"Second place goes to Justin Peterson for his tornado chamber."

More applause. Eddy concentrated on his ribbon. He had wanted the blue one.

"And the winner is Keisha Davis with her working model of the human digestive system." Keisha squealed and jogged to the stage to get her blue ribbon, smiling and waving. The applause was louder.

It wasn't fair. Eddy knew his project should have won. His eddy coil had performed flawlessly.

A very loud noise ("Let's have a round of applause for all of our future scientists!") signaled the end of the award announcements.

Eddy made his way back to his exhibit and threw his eddy coil back into the cardboard box he had brought it in.

"What's the matter?" asked Dad.

"Third."

"Third is good. You'll be the alternate."

"Big deal. I should have won. I will not get to go to regionals."

"I'm not really surprised you didn't come in first. It wasn't your best work. The coil itself was great, but you didn't explain it very well."

"I did not have enough time," whined Eddy.

"You would have had enough time if you hadn't wasted all that time unwinding and rewinding your coil."

"I wanted it to be just right," said Eddy. "It had to be perfect."

"And it was perfect, but the poster could have used some more work."

"Do we have to talk about this now?" Eddy shouted. He turned away from his father and dropped the transformer into the box, on top of the eddy coil. Then he felt something being pulled off the back of his shirt.

"What is that?" asked Eddy.

"Nothing," replied his father, trying unsuccessfully to hide a piece of paper in his pocket. Eddy grabbed the paper. In big bold letters, it said I AM A GEEK.

"Was that thing on my back when I went up onstage?" asked Eddy.

"Well … yeah," mumbled Dad.

"Did you see who did it this time?"

"No. Sorry."

Eddy growled. He ripped down his poster, rolled it up, and shoved it into the box. It didn't fit, so he smashed it down. Without another word to his father, he picked up the box, leaving the third-place ribbon on the table.

Fact Number 3.14159 from the Random Access Memory of Edison Thomas: The loudest noise ever heard by human ears (in recorded history) was the eruption of the volcano Krakatoa in Indonesia on August 27, 1883. The sound was heard three thousand miles away, and shock waves from the explosion circled the earth seven times.

Eddy plodded home, a cold rain dripping down the back of his neck. Water seeped into his sneakers, and the box he was carrying was getting soggy. He quickened his pace, knowing his dad wouldn't be able to keep up.

"Eddy!"

Dad could yell all he wanted. Nothing he could say would make Eddy feel better.

"Eddy!"

As he stepped into the street, Eddy hopped over the stream of water rushing down the gutter toward the storm sewer. A car horn honked. Eddy stepped back quickly as a car swerved to miss him. He stood with his foot in the gutter, feeling the water seep between his toes as the car drove away.

Dad finally caught up. "What were you thinking?"

"Nothing."

"Apparently. I wish you would use that head of yours for something besides holding up your hat."

Eddy pulled his foot out of the water and proceeded to walk home, his shoe squishing with every step. As usual, Dad wasn't making any sense. Eddy wasn't even wearing a hat.

2. Good-bye, Adios, Chow Chow

At 6:30:00 a.m., Eddy's Wake-Upper kicked in. He had gotten the timer from a coffeemaker, the kind that has your coffee ready when you wake up. The CD of ocean waves that had been playing all night faded slowly into silence. At the same time, another CD player containing a CD by his favorite group, They Might Be Giants, began to play a song called "Photosynthesis". The volume started very low and gradually increased. His bedside lamp began to get brighter. By 6:33:00 a.m., the CD and lamp were at full intensity.

Eddy was awake, but still calm. The Wake-Upper worked much better than his old alarm clock with the loud buzzer. The buzzer woke him up, but he would sit bolt upright with a racing heart. Not a good way to start the day.

After a trip to the bathroom, he checked the day's schedule, which he had printed out the previous night and taped to the door.

Today is Friday, October 6. Check.

Pee. Check.

Get dressed: Blue jeans, black NASA T-shirt, Woolman College sweatshirt. Check.

Eddy got dressed, took the schedule off the door, folded it, and put it in the right rear pocket of his jeans. The schedule worked pretty well, except when he forgot to take it out of his pocket to check it.

Eddy missed his electronic organizer. He could check his schedule weeks ahead of time. He could also keep track of homework assignments and write notes to himself. That was the problem. He could do so much with his electronic organizer that he wasted too much time fiddling with it. (Why do they call it fiddling when it has nothing to do with violins?) He had made the mistake of fiddling with it in social studies, and Mr. Adler took it away.

Eddy's breakfast, as usual, consisted of cornflakes, a banana (*Musa balbisiana*), milk (1 percent), and orange juice (calcium-fortified). His mom emerged from her studio, a pencil behind her ear and ink smudges on her face. She refilled her oversized coffee cup shaped like a squirrel (*Sciurus carolinensis*), with the tail for a handle. She sat down next to Eddy and asked, "What's on your schedule for today?"

Eddy pulled his schedule out of his pocket. "Looks pretty good. Math test, session with Tiffany, report on Battle of Bunker Hill due—"

"Did you finish the report?" interrupted Dad, plopping his spoon down into his oatmeal, which appeared especially viscous this morning.

"Almost," said Eddy. "I will finish it at lunch."

"ALMOST?" laughed Dad. "Do you really expect to finish it at lunch? You're lucky if you finish your lunch at lunch."

"Jeff, that's enough," chided Mom. "There's nothing he can do about it now. Eddy, you'd better get going. Don't forget your lunch."

Eddy didn't forget his lunch. He did, however, forget to put his schedule back in his pocket.

Fact Number 9,192,631,770 from the Random Access Memory of Edison Thomas: In the past, time was measured based on Earth's rotation. Modern atomic clocks are so accurate that, in 1967, scientists redefined the second based on the vibrations of a cesium-133 atom.

On the walk to school, Eddy brooded about the science fair. Alternate. Big deal. He would not have the opportunity to bring his eddy coil to the regional science competition. Unless … unless, for any reason, the first- or second-place finisher was unable to attend. What would make someone unable to attend the regionals? Nothing would keep Eddy away, except maybe death. It was probably wrong to hope for the death of Keisha Davis or Justin Peterson. Illness, perhaps? Kidnapping? A jail sentence?

As he reached the corner of Delaware Avenue and Hatteras Street, he heard a deep voice. "Gooood morning!" bellowed Jim, the crossing guard. "How are you today?"

"Fine," replied Eddy.

"Watch your step," said Jim as he walked into the street with his hand-held stop sign. "It rained cats and dogs last night, and you wouldn't want to step in a POODLE."

Eddy stepped into the street, snickering. Raining *Felis silvestris* and *Canis familiaris*. That was pretty funny.

"I think you'll be all right, though," added Jim as Eddy passed by. "I can only see MINIATURE POODLES."

Eddy reached the other side of the street.

"Here's a POINTER for you. If you get cold, you could wrap yourself in an AFGHAN HOUND!"

"Right," said Eddy.

"Well, CHOW CHOW for now!" yelled Jim as Eddy walked away. "I'll see you this afternoon. Have a GREAT DANE!"

Fact Number 5,280 from the Random Access Memory of Edison Thomas: Sled dogs are the world's most powerful draft animals; a team of sled dogs can pull the same weight as a team of horses weighing twice as much. Winning teams can run the Iditarod, a 1,150-mile sled dog race from Anchorage to Nome, Alaska, in about nine days.

Eddy realized he had forgotten his schedule as soon as he sat down at his desk in homeroom. For the rest of the morning, he had been repeating what he could remember of the schedule over and over in his head so he wouldn't forget anything. Today was a Tiffany day. Usually that was a good thing, but since he didn't want to forget about his appointment with Tiffany, he was having trouble concentrating on the task at hand—the math test.

He looked up at the clock on the wall. 10:38. Sometimes

it seemed as if the clock wasn't moving. He listened for the click as the minute hand of the clock moved to the next minute. 10:39. It was probably just slow. He looked at his watch. 10:39:47. The chances of his watch and the clock showing the exact same time, but both being wrong, were pretty small.

Eddy nearly jumped out of his seat when Ms. Johnson tapped him on the shoulder and said quietly, "You've only got ten minutes to finish up. I suggest you stop daydreaming and get to work."

Eddy looked down at his work. The math was easy. The hard part was writing down the numbers. He had finished only four problems. He checked those answers for flip-overs. It looked pretty good, with only one backward six and two backward fours. He erased those and rewrote them, checking them against the numbers that were already printed on the page to make sure he wrote them the right way around. He took a deep breath and tried to focus his mind on the math, pushing other thoughts out of his head. He had to finish before Tiffany arrived.

At 10:49:42, Tiffany popped her head into the room. "Ready?" she asked.

"Almost," said Eddy as he wrote the last number, put his pencil away, and stood up to bring the paper to Ms. Johnson.

As Eddy walked with Tiffany to her office, he listened to the clicking of her fancy pointed shoes echoing in the hall. Eddy always wore quiet shoes. Eddy liked it when he and

Tiffany were the only people in the hall. Between classes, there were so many other people, he couldn't hear the individual footsteps. They got all mixed up into one big noise.

"How was your math test?" asked Tiffany.

"Fine," said Eddy.

"How are your numbers?"

"Good."

"Not as many flip-overs?"

"No, I just compare the numbers I write to the ones that are already on the page."

"What if there are no numbers already there?"

"Then I look at the clock. All the numbers are there."

"Good strategy," said Tiffany.

Fact Number 305 from the Random Access Memory of Edison Thomas: In the fourteenth century, shoemakers began to make shoes to fit either the right or left foot. Before that, right and left shoes were identical.

Eddy's session with Tiffany took longer than it should have. Tiffany had some new computer software that showed video clips of famous actors and actresses in movies. Eddy had to decide what emotions they were showing. He did fine with the scenes from movies in his own collection of science fiction and fantasy DVDs but had to guess at the unfamiliar ones, and the harder he tried, the worse he did. He didn't want to leave until he had reached level two, but Tiffany finally convinced him that he needed to quit.

As always, Eddy tensed up when he entered the lunch-room, trying to defend his brain from the onslaught of noise and smells and the visual clutter of hundreds of kids. He preferred to sit in the corner of the room, which was quieter and had walls instead of people on two sides. Unfortunately, he was so late today that his usual corner was not available.

It looked like a spot was open at Mitch's table, even though three girls he didn't recognize had joined the usual lunchtime trio of Mitch, Will, and Mark. Mitch sure had a lot of friends.

"Hey, Mitch," said Eddy. "Can I sit with you?"

"Sorry, Professor, that seat is saved," replied Mitch.

"Yeah, for humans," muttered Mark. The girls giggled.

"Maybe some other time," said Mitch. "I see some seats on the other side of the room. Waaaaay over there."

"Thank you," said Eddy. He turned, stumbled slightly, and walked away. He heard Will mumble something that sounded to Eddy like *Homo sapiens*, and the girls giggled again.

Eddy made his way to the other side of the room, but he didn't see any open spots. He did see Keisha Davis, first-place finisher at the science fair. She was laughing with some friends, obviously pleased with herself. No room for Eddy there. He stood looking for a place to sit, trying not to panic, when a voice came from behind him.

"There's room at my table, Eddy."

He turned to see a small kid with messy hair the color of sandstone and large glasses to match. He recognized him from the science fair. Was this the kid that put the GEEK note on Eddy's back? Eddy was too hungry to care at the moment, so he sat down and started to eat his lunch.

"My name is Justin Peterson," said the boy.

"Eddy Thomas," said Eddy.

"I know. Congratulations on finishing third in the science fair," said Justin.

Eddy grunted as he chewed on his sandwich—peanut butter (chunky) and honey (also known as bee vomit) on whole wheat (stone ground). He didn't want to be reminded of his failure.

"What would happen if the ring was made of a metal besides copper?" asked Justin.

"Nonferrous metals, like aluminum, would be repelled by the induced field, just like copper," explained Eddy. "But ferrous metals like iron or steel or nickel would be attracted."

"Like they would be attracted to a magnet."

"Exactly. In that case, the coil would be acting as an electromagnet." Eddy bit into his apple (*Malus domestica*, variety Macintosh).

"So ... Eddy." Justin hesitated. "Did you get to see my project, the tornado chamber?"

Eddy remembered that Justin had won second place with his project, a pan of hot water in the bottom of an acrylic box. Slits in the side of the box let the cold air in, forming a vortex that resembled a tornado. Justin's project was good, but not as spectacular as the eddy coil. Eddy could have done a better job on the tornado chamber. He would have rigged it so that the temperature gradient was steeper. That would produce more water vapor and make the tornado much more impressive.

"I got most of the pictures of damage caused by tornadoes with different Fujita scale ratings from the Internet," continued Justin. "Except for that F5 storm in 1984 in Barneveld, Wisconsin. My great-aunt Lena lives right near there and took those pictures. She says the tornado wiped out 90 percent of the town."

Eddy wished Justin would stop rubbing it in. Justin was going to regionals and Eddy was not. Maybe Justin would drop out.

Justin paused. "Listen, I think it really stinks that somebody did that to you at the science fair. That note on your back. Do you have any idea who did it?"

Why would Justin ask that? "Was it you?" asked Eddy.

Justin laughed. "Me? Why would I call you a geek? That would be like the pot calling the kettle black."

The bell rang before Eddy could ask Justin what cooking utensils had to do with anything.

"Snap! I have to run," said Justin, shoving what was left of his lunch into his backpack. "I promised Ms. Copeland I would help her set up the microscopes."

Eddy didn't finish his report on Bunker Hill at lunch. He didn't even have time to finish his lunch. Again.

Fact Number 695 from the Random Access Memory of Edison Thomas: The Enhanced Fujita scale was adopted on

February 1, 2007, and rates the intensity of tornadoes, ranging from EF0 to EF5. It replaced the Fujita scale, which ranged from F0 to F6 (although an F6 tornado has never been recorded). Tornadoes are classified based on the damage they do, not on direct measurement of wind speed.

When he crossed the street on his way home, Eddy heard Jim speak to him as he passed.

"Well, I guess this is good-bye, my friend," said Jim.

"Good-bye," replied Eddy. "I will see you on Monday."

"No, I'm afraid you won't."

Eddy got to the other side of the street, paused, and turned to face Jim. "I do not understand."

"I've been laid off," said Jim. "The city cut the budget, and my job was one of the cuts. They figure that since there's a stop sign at this intersection, I'm not really needed."

Eddy didn't like this. He liked Jim. He didn't like change.

"It's OK, really," continued Jim. "I'm getting too old for this. I'm going to like staying inside when the weather's bad. Nothing like putting your feet up with a nice cup of hot cocoa."

Jim had been the crossing guard at this corner since Eddy was in first grade.

"I don't think it will be a problem for the middle-schoolers, but I worry about the little kids. The city must realize that I'm the crossing guard for both schools."

Visions of first-graders, like his neighbor Lily Mae, struck by cars began to form in Eddy's head.

Jim was still talking. "Yeah, today is my last day. You'll have to do something else to keep yourself entertained on the way to school. I won't be able to crack you up with my razor-sharp wit anymore."

Crack. Razor. Eddy needed to think. He shoved his hands into his pockets, turned, and walked away.

"It's been nice knowin' you!" Jim yelled after him.

Eddy took giant steps and studied the cracks in the sidewalk as he passed over each one. Crack. Razor. Crack. Razor. He concentrated on the sidewalk cracks and tried to get the image of a razor out of his head. Crack, crack, crack. His rhythmic walking had a calming effect as he placed each foot heavily on the ground and felt the pressure in his legs. He timed his breathing to match his stride.

As he felt calmer, he started to look at things besides the sidewalk. On the right was a dog turd someone had neglected to pick up. He veered left.

Treasure on the left. Someone was moving out of the little brick house on Nanticoke Street. He would have to come back later with his wagon to harvest the discarded fruits of a cleared-out attic.

3. The Mother Load

"Gooood Morning, Eddy," said Jim. "And how are you this fine morning?"

"Ummm, fine," replied Eddy, puzzled to see Jim at his usual spot on the corner of Delaware Avenue and Hatteras Street.

"Here's one you'll like," said Jim. "What's the metric equivalent of a pound cake?"

"I give up. What?"

"450 graham crackers. Get it? GRAM crackers?"

"To be more precise, there are 453.59237 grams in a pound."

"I can always count on you for precision, Eddy."

"You told me you were not coming back," said Eddy as Jim walked to the center of the street with his hand-held stop sign.

"I went to the city and told them that if they laid me off someone would inevitably be hurt or even killed," said Jim.

"And they gave you your job back?"

"Hard to believe, isn't it? I guess you really can fight City Hall."

Eddy imagined Jim striding up the steps of the

municipal building in boxing gloves. His thoughts were interrupted by the sound of a truck horn. He looked to his right and saw a huge moving van barreling down the road, straight at Jim, who didn't seem to notice.

"Jim!" yelled Eddy. "Get out of the road!"

Jim didn't budge. He stood there laughing as the truck got closer … and closer. The horn got louder and louder as the truck seemed to be speeding up. Jim just stood there, smiling.

"Jim!" yelled Eddy. "JIM! WATCH OUT!"

Eddy sat up suddenly in bed. His hair felt as if he'd just come out of the shower, and sweat dripped into his ears. His heart rate was elevated, and he was breathing heavily. He looked around his dark bedroom. It took a few seconds for him to realize he had been dreaming. He laid his head back down, but his pillow was drenched with sweat. He turned it over and tried to think about something pleasant. Something that had nothing to do with trucks. He turned up the volume on his *Ocean Dreams* CD. He tried to picture waves crashing onto the shore instead of cars and trucks crashing into people, but it was no use. He stared up at the astronomically correct glow-in-the dark stars on his ceiling, cars crashing in his head, until 6:30:00 a.m., when his Wake-Upper kicked in with They Might Be Giants singing "I Am a Paleontologist."

Fact Number 350 from the Random Access Memory of Edison Thomas: The world's largest truck, the Terex Titan, has tires eleven feet in diameter.

The dream of Jim and the moving van kept playing over and over in Eddy's head like a video clip, even while he ate his cornflakes. It wasn't until his mom asked him what he had planned for the day that he remembered the wonderful pile of stuff on the curb on Nanticoke Street. Finally, he had something he could concentrate on hard enough to chase away Jim's image. He finished breakfast quickly, went out back for his wagon, and embarked on his treasure hunt.

Eddy loved it when people moved. All that stuff they keep around for years suddenly doesn't seem worth the trouble of packing into a box or loading into a truck. College students were especially good at leaving perfectly useful stuff. The best time for trash hunting was at the end of the school year. During last year's Dumpster-diving season, Eddy harvested a vacuum cleaner, two microwaves, and a laptop computer. He wasn't sure if the laptop was intended to be trash; it was a little outdated, but still perfectly serviceable. With a little tweaking, it had become Eddy's new favorite computer.

Eddy's dad was a great tweaker. He worked as an electrician at Woolman College and his job was to fix all the equipment that went "on the blink." (Eddy always thought that was a strange expression. Broken equipment seldom blinks, although some electronic devices display a blinking error message.) The best part of Dad's job was first dibs on the unfixably broken or hopelessly obsolete equipment that was to be thrown away.

Dad had brought home an old overhead projector

from the Math Department, a pH meter from the Biology Department, and a lighting board from the Theater Department. He knew that Eddy could always come up with a creative use for discarded machines. They were full of parts that could be salvaged and reused in one of Eddy's inventions.

Eddy made five trips to the junk pile on the curb at Nanticoke Street. He could see Jim's corner in the distance every time he approached the pile, but the lure of junk kept him from thinking about it too much.

He had picked up some great old mechanical things: an adding machine, a check printer, and a wind-up alarm clock with two bells on the top. Newer machines with electronic components were all right, but they were not as interesting as the older stuff, which contained all kinds of gears and pulleys and motors and flywheels.

As he was loading up his wagon for the sixth time, a tall man in faded blue coveralls walked down the driveway toward Eddy, carrying a very heavy box. Eddy froze, his hands clutching an electric mixer with one bent beater. Would this man yell at him for taking stuff from the pile?

"You live in this neighborhood?" asked the man, setting down the box, which Eddy now saw was full of old *National Geographic* magazines.

"Yes, on Cherokee Road," said Eddy, relieved. "May I take some of this junk?"

"Go ahead. None of it works, though," said the man. He ran his fingers through his curly hair, which was covered with dust and cobwebs so that it resembled brown banded agate.

"It does not matter," said Eddy. "I am just going to take it apart."

"Suit yourself. There's plenty more where that came from."

"You really should recycle those magazines," said Eddy. "Instead of taking up space in the landfill, magazines can be converted to pulp and made into new paper. In fact, newspaper recyclers need magazines. The addition of magazine pulp to newspaper pulp raises the pH and makes it easier to remove the ink."

"Fine," said the man, and he turned around without another word. Eddy stood still for a moment and watched the man walk back up the driveway. Sometimes conversations were more trouble than they were worth. He loaded his wagon up with a toaster, a blender, a camera with a broken lens, a sewing machine, a VCR, and a metal detector.

Fact Number 700 from the Random Access Memory of Edison Thomas: Paper makes up 40 percent of the contents of municipal landfills in the United States.

After another restless night full of images of Jim and various large motor vehicles, Eddy spent Sunday in the basement, disassembling some of his new acquisitions. His current project was a microwave oven. He had just finished taking out its hidden treasures, two extra-strong circular magnets. Eddy had collected forty-six magnets so far. The magnets were so powerful that he had to be careful not to let his fingers get pinched between two of them. His mom wouldn't let him use them on the fridge because they were so hard to pull off, you had to slide them to the edge of the refrigerator, scratching the door. Unlike the cheap little squirrel-shaped magnets his mom collected, one microwave magnet could hold up a whole calendar.

Eddy loved taking things apart, not only because he liked to salvage the parts for his inventions, but also because a good, complex disassembly task could dominate his thoughts. At this particular moment, he could concentrate on the locking mechanism for the microwave door so that he didn't have to think about the potentially disastrous consequences of Jim losing his crossing guard job.

Tiffany was always getting on Eddy's case because of how much time he spent alone in his basement. She thought he should spend more time hanging out with other kids. He tried asking Mitch a couple of times if he wanted to come over, but Mitch was always too busy.

Tha-thunk. Tha-thunk. Dad's work boots tramped down the basement steps with Dad's typical uneven gait. "You've been down here all day," said Dad, kicking the discarded shell of the microwave oven out of the way as he entered the workshop. "It's almost time for dinner. Don't you have any homework to do?"

"Just a little math," replied Eddy without looking up from the circuit board he was now trying to dislodge. "Oh, and I need to decide on a famous person to write a biography about for English class."

"How about your namesake?"

Eddy's screwdriver slipped and he scratched his finger on the edge of the circuit board. "Thomas Edison? Why did you have to give me such a stupid name?" he growled, putting his finger in his mouth to clean the blood off of it.

"It's an important Thomas family tradition," said Dad. He started rummaging through the top drawer of his tool chest. "Maybe you'll grow up to be a famous inventor."

"You did not grow up to be president like Thomas Jefferson."

"Neither did my cousin Wilson."

"Wilson Thomas? There was no president named Thomas Wilson," insisted Eddy.

"Ah, but that's where you're wrong. It's a little-known fact that Woodrow Wilson's real first name was Thomas."

"So neither you nor your cousin became president."

"Yeah, well sometimes our names fit us and sometimes they don't. Your uncle Paine Thomas, for example, turned out to be a genuine pain, but your aunt Aquinas Thomas is no saint." Dad closed the top drawer and opened the next drawer down. "I have a feeling you are aptly named."

"That is not a good reason to do my project on Thomas Edison."

"You and he have a lot in common."

"We both invent things."

"I think you'll find that there's more to life than inventions. Give Edison a chance. You'll thank me for it."

"I do not think so."

Dad started looking in the third drawer of his tool chest. He stopped suddenly and looked at Eddy. "What was I looking for?"

"I do not know." Dad often expected Eddy to read his mind, which is technically impossible.

"Well, finish up and come upstairs for dinner. I made lasagna."

"With garlic bread?"

"You bet."

"I will just be a little while. I am almost finished with this." The screw he was working on wasn't budging. Time for the hacksaw.

"Five minutes, understand?" said Dad.

"Understood."

Eddy put down his screwdriver and studied what was left of the microwave. He still wanted to get at the motor that drove the turntable.

Before any time seemed to have passed, the light on Eddy's intercom flashed. He had modified the intercom the previous week. The light flashed three seconds before any sound could come through, letting him prepare himself so he wasn't startled by the noise.

"Eddy, dinner's on the table," came his father's voice. Eddy realized he was very hungry, not having eaten anything since breakfast (cornflakes, banana, milk, OJ).

He charged up the stairs, washed his hands, and sat at the table in time to call dibs on both noses. The noses, the crunchy end pieces of the garlic bread, were the best part of Dad's lasagna dinners. His mom liked them, too, but luckily, Mom was late to the table because she had tried (unsuccessfully) to scrub the purple and green ink stains from her hands.

"Hey," said Eddy after he had wolfed down the second nose. "I have a joke for you."

"Fire away," said Dad.

A picture of smoking cannons on the deck of a pirate ship came to Eddy's head.

"Eddy," prompted Mom. "The joke?"

"Oh, yes. A ship is sailing off the coast of Madagascar. The captain looks through his telescope and sees a strange animal. It is a primate with prominent eyes, large ears, and one very long finger on each of its forepaws. He calls to his science officer, 'What is that strange animal?' and the science officer says, 'Aye-aye, Captain.'"

Silence.

"Aye-aye. Get it?" said Eddy.

"Oh, was that it?" asked Dad.

"It was very funny, dear," said Mom, but she wasn't laughing. This confused Eddy.

"Aye-aye," repeated Eddy. "It is a kind of lemur, *Daubentonia madagascariensis*. The aye-aye. I guess I need to work on that one."

"I guess so," agreed Dad.

Mom changed the subject. "Eddy, I want you to clean your rabbit's cage tonight. It's really getting disgusting."

"All right," said Eddy with his mouth full.

"Did you ever give that rabbit a name?" asked Dad.

Eddy took a drink of milk. "Yes," he said. "*Oryctolagus cuniculus.*"

"I mean a real name, not a scientific one," said Dad. "How about 'Tank Engine'?"

"What?"

"You know, Tank Engine Thomas. You used to love Thomas the Tank Engine."

"I was four years old," growled Eddy. "*Oryctolagus cuniculus* is fine."

"Just trying to uphold family tradition," said Dad.

"You know, Jeff," said Mom, "I think this tradition has been upheld long enough."

Eddy couldn't have agreed more.

4. Playing Ketchup

In the morning, Eddy could see Jim's corner from three blocks away. He was relieved to see that Jim wasn't there. He was safe, out of reach of the trucks that threatened him every night in Eddy's dreams.

By the time Eddy reached the corner, he had counted five cars (out of twenty-five cars passing through the intersection) that did not come to a complete stop at the stop sign. A full 20 percent were breaking the law while kids were walking to school. How many drivers ignored the stop sign at other times of the day? Eddy's nightmares stood a good chance of actually coming true, but Jim would not be the only one in danger. Children could be hurt, or even killed.

Eddy took a deep breath and looked left, then right, then left again. Then he looked right, then left, then right again. Then, just to be sure, he looked left, then right, and then left again. He crossed as quickly as he could.

Fact Number 75 from the Random Access Memory of Edison Thomas: In countries where vehicles drive on the left side of the road (including Japan and the United Kingdom), collisions are less likely than in countries where traffic keeps to the right (including the United States and France).

—

Eddy hoped math class would be just the thing to occupy his brain enough to keep Jim away. Ms. Johnson was handing back the tests from Friday, and an A could always cheer him up. He liked it when she whispered "Nice job, Eddy" to him as she handed back math homework and tests. This time she didn't say anything as she placed his test paper face-down on his desk.

Eddy turned the paper over. At the top, in red ink, was a big, fat B+.

Eddy was stunned. He had known every answer. He checked every problem. Every answer was correct. How could he have failed to get an A? His test paper was perfect, just like his eddy coil had been. So why didn't he get a perfect score?

He looked at the paper again, trying to find a clue. Under the B+, embedded in the instructions printed at the top of the page, was a red circle (actually, it was more of an ellipse) around the words *Show your work.*

He looked up at Ms. Johnson, who was writing some equations on the board. He wanted to raise his hand and ask for clarification but decided not to interrupt the lesson. Instead, he looked over his test. Continuously. Until the bell rang for lunch.

Fact Number 343 from the Random Access Memory of Edison Thomas: If the air is removed from a chamber that contains a ringing bell, the bell will no longer make a sound.

Eddy got to the lunchroom in time to sit in his favorite spot in the corner. He pulled his math test out of his pocket and stared at it, trying to figure out how to show work he didn't do.

"Do you mind if I sit with you?" said Justin as he sat down next to Eddy.

Eddy didn't particularly feel like sitting with Justin, but he didn't say anything. He was used to sitting alone, or at least effectively alone. He was often in close physical proximity to kids at lunch, but conversations were rare. Why did Justin want to sit with him? To gloat about the fact that he was going to the regional science fair and Eddy wasn't?

"That was a really tough test," said Justin, unpacking his sandwich.

Eddy hadn't realized that Justin was in his class. He grunted.

"Didn't you think it was hard?" asked Justin, taking a bite of his sandwich.

"Not really," replied Eddy. "But I got points taken off for not showing my work." Eddy's stomach began to squirm, as if a giant anaconda (*Eunectes murinus*) had been coiled up there sleeping and suddenly woke up and shifted position. Somebody in the lunchroom was eating fish.

"Ms. Johnson is a real stickler for showing work." Justin's mouth was full.

"I know, but I showed all the work I did," protested Eddy. "I do not know how I could have shown more."

"Let's have a look." Justin snatched the paper out of Eddy's hand. "Here, for instance, number 3. That one was complicated. You should have written down the intermediate steps."

"What intermediate steps? I wrote down everything."

"Holy snap! You're not telling me you did that in your head!" Justin's mouth gaped open.

Eddy could see traces of Justin's sandwich stuck between his teeth. It smelled like tuna (*Thunnus alalunga*). That explained Eddy's upset stomach.

"Sure." Eddy shrugged.

"How?"

"I just see it in my head."

"Like the numbers on a calculator?"

"Not really." Eddy paused to think. He had never tried to explain how he did math. "Things just sort of group themselves into patterns in my head and I rearrange them. Everyone does it that way, right?"

"Well, I sure don't."

They ate their sandwiches in silence for a while. Eddy had peanut butter and bee vomit, as always. The smell of Justin's tuna sandwich was making him extremely queasy. He tried to think of something else, but soon he lost his appetite and set his sandwich down, just as Mitch Cooper and Will Pease approached the table.

"Hey, Professor," said Will. "Can you settle a bet for us?"

"Certainly," said Eddy. "What can I do for you?"

"Mitch says ketchup would work better in a water pistol than mustard, but I think mustard would work better. What do you think?"

"Neither one would work in a water gun. The diameter of the nozzle is too narrow. It would take too much pressure to squeeze it out. If you want, I could design a gun that would accommodate a more viscous fluid."

"That would be great!" said Mitch. He leaned in way too close to Eddy's face. Eddy smelled pepperoni on his breath. "Make me a ketchup gun and make Will a mustard gun. That would be better than paintball."

"And tastier," added Will.

"We'll see you later," said Mitch hastily, leaving a paper bag on the table in front of Eddy as he and Will walked quickly away.

"What's in the bag?" asked Justin. "Did Mitch forget his lunch?"

Eddy peeked into the bag. It was full of packets of the condiments that went along with the hot lunches—ketchup, mustard, mayonnaise, taco sauce, and salad dressing. Eddy looked around for Mitch and Will, but they had disappeared into the lunchroom crowd.

"They probably took those from ...," said Justin.

Eddy was still thinking about the bet. Mustard (made from the seed of *Brassica hirta*) is more viscous than ketchup in general. Mayonnaise is probably even thicker but contains more oil. What could he use to build a ketchup gun? He would need to design a pumping mechanism that would apply more pressure than your standard water gun. It should have a longer trigger stroke but narrower plunger diameter.

"... think they're so cool ...," continued Justin.

Eddy picked up a packet and squeezed it between his fingers, feeling the ketchup goosh from side to side. He tried to rip a little corner off the packet. Then he tried to bite off a corner. He hated these packets. They were always so hard to open.

"… you really shouldn't …"

Eddy squeezed the packet in his fist and felt the ketchup push back against his fingers and strain against the seams of the packet. He threw the ketchup packet down on the table and raised his fist.

"Eddy!"

He brought his fist down on the ketchup packet. Hard. As soon as he did it, he knew he shouldn't have. Not only because it would make a mess, which it did, or because he would get in trouble, which he probably would, but also because of the high-pitched shriek that hurt his ears.

He looked up at the source of the shriek: a red-haired girl wearing a white sweater with one ketchup-colored sleeve.

Fact Number 1,893 from the Random Access Memory of Edison Thomas: Even though tomatoes (*Lycopersicon esculentum*) are associated with Italian food, tomatoes are native to South America and were not introduced to Europe until the early 1500s.

5. Alva and Edison

"Welcome back, Eddy," said Mr. Benton. "It's been weeks since you've visited me in my office. Come on in."

Eddy never *visited* Mr. Benton. He got sent to his office when he was in trouble. Mr. Benton had a confusing way of saying things.

"Sit down," said Mr. Benton.

Eddy sat in a very hard yellow chair.

"Do you have anything to say, Eddy?"

"Not really," replied Eddy. Mr. Benton sure had a lot of certificates on the wall of his office.

"Look at me when I'm talking to you, please."

Eddy didn't like looking at people's eyes, so he looked at Mr. Benton's mouth. A piece of food clung to his top left incisor— lettuce (*Lactuca sativa*) or maybe spinach (*Spinacia oleracea*).

"Do you know why you're here?"

"Because I am in trouble?"

"Smart kid. Do you think it might have anything to do with ketchup?"

"Probably."

"Well, let me refresh your memory. Miss McCabe tells me—"

"Who?" asked Eddy. Who was Miss McCabe? A teacher?

He didn't know any teachers named Miss McCabe.

"Meara McCabe. She says the sweater you … shall we say … decorated was very expensive and has great sentimental value."

Eddy remembered now. Meara had red hair, which was actually an orange color compared with the ketchup on her sleeve. No, not really orange. More like the color of freshly polished copper.

"What do you intend to do about it?" asked Mr. Benton.

"Club soda will remove many stains. It is mildly acidic, and the dissolved mineral salts will—"

"Thank you for the science lesson."

"You are welcome," replied Eddy.

Mr. Benton let out a sigh. "We'll just let the dry cleaners take care of the stain, won't we? Is there anything else you can do?"

"Apologize?" That was always a good answer to try while sitting in the principal's office.

"I think you can do better than that," said Mr. Benton through clenched teeth.

"Apologize profusely?" suggested Eddy.

"Here's a hint. I think it would be appropriate for you to pay the dry-cleaning bill." Mr. Benton's hands were now clenched into fists, which probably meant that he was angry, or maybe frustrated. Eddy decided not to say much more, since Mr. Benton seemed to be getting mad at him no matter what he said.

"Very well."

"And detention is also warranted."

"Understood."

"I trust you will be able to control yourself in the lunch-room in the future?"

"I will try."

"Good," said Mr. Benton. "Now get back to class. Stop by Ms. Yamada's desk on your way out so you can schedule your detention."

"I will."

"It's always a pleasure to see you, Eddy. Let's not do it again real soon."

Fact Number 32 from the Random Access Memory of Edison Thomas: Tooth enamel is the hardest substance in the human body.

Eddy's head felt scattered and noisy. On his way back to class from Mr. Benton's office, he took a detour past the gym. He peeked into Coach Vang's office.

Coach Vang looked up from his paperwork. "Need some tramp time?" he asked.

Eddy nodded silently. Coach Vang got up and unlocked the storage room adjacent to his office. "Knock yourself out," he said.

"I will be careful not to knock myself out," replied Eddy as he walked into the storage room. There, in among the basketballs, orange plastic cones, and tennis rackets, was a trampoline, one meter in diameter. Eddy stepped on it and began jumping, vigorously at first. He pounded his feet into the fabric with every jump. After a while, he settled into a rhythm. A feeling of calm spread up his legs, through his torso, and eventually to his head. He continued jumping rhythmically, the springs of the trampoline squeaking in time with every jump.

Coach Vang popped his head into the storage room to remind Eddy to get back to class.

Reluctantly, Eddy stopped jumping and stepped off the trampoline. He knew he needed to go, but he couldn't wait for the afternoon to be over so he could go down to his basement and take apart a VCR.

Fact Number 211,646 from the Random Access Memory of Edison Thomas: The first modern trampoline was made in 1934 by Larry Griswold and George Nissen, who named it after the Spanish word for diving board, *trampolín*.

Over the next few days, thoughts of the traffic situation at the corner of Delaware and Hatteras took up more and more of Eddy's thinking time. Every day he counted at least ten cars that failed to come to a complete stop at the stop sign. There were usually more offenders in the morning than in the afternoon. Another thing he noticed was that the drivers who ran the stop sign tended to be talking on cell phones. No matter how hard he tried to concentrate on something else, the intersection was always in his brain.

Fact Number 0.08 from the Random Access Memory of Edison Thomas: Drivers talking on cell phones have worse reflexes than people who are legally drunk.

Over the next few nights, Eddy's subconscious took over and the nightmares continued. In fact, they were getting worse. They still had the same theme: pedestrians struck by cars and trucks. Only now, young children, like his first-grade neighbor, Lily Mae, were sent flying through the air like rag dolls. He often had two or more nightmares per night, soaking his pillow with sweat. This was a problem, because he could turn his pillow over and sleep on the dry side if he had one nightmare, but if he had another, both sides of his pillow would be wet, and he had to get up, go to the linen closet in the hall, and get a fresh pillowcase. The lack of sleep caused by the repeated dreams of Jim and Lily Mae in danger had reduced his ability to concentrate on other things during his waking hours. He couldn't get that image of flying rag-doll children out of his mind.

Fact Number 264 from the Random Access Memory of Edison Thomas: Prolonged periods of sleep deprivation may result in blurred vision, nausea, confusion, headache, dizziness, and hallucinations.

On Thursday, Justin sat with Eddy at lunch again. Eddy had his usual, *Arachis hypogaea* butter and *Apis mellifera* vomit on whole *Triticum aestivum* bread. Justin had *Thunnus alalunga* again. The smell of Justin's tuna sandwich seeped steadily into Eddy's consciousness, expanding and crowding out other sensations, including the usual noise of the lunchroom. He tried to concentrate on his own sandwich.

Eddy nearly dropped his sandwich because of a surprisingly hard pat on the back.

"Well, if it isn't Captain Ketchup," said Mitch. He was with his friends Mark and Will. "Have you invented a new high-tech way to shoot ketchup across the room, or are you going to stick with your fist?"

"I have not quite figured out a design for a ketchup gun," replied Eddy. "But I could fabricate one in about a week, if you want." The truth was that he hadn't even thought about the ketchup gun, because his mind had been occupied by the traffic situation at Jim's corner. He hoped Mitch would understand.

Mark punched Will on the arm and burst out into a laugh that hurt Eddy's ears.

"That's OK," said Mitch. "I think I proved my point."

Will roared with laughter as they walked away. Eddy forced himself to take a few more bites of his sandwich. If he kept smelling Justin's tuna fish much longer, he wouldn't be able to eat any more.

"Why do you put up with that snap?" asked Justin.

"Huh?" said Eddy.

"Why do you let them do that to you?"

"Do what?"

"Get you in trouble."

"I am just helping them out with an invention."

"There's no invention. They're just trying to get you to do stupid stuff. And it works."

"What do you mean?"

"Mitch and Will wanted you to make that ketchup mess and get in trouble. That's why they left the bag of ketchup packets and asked you about water pistols."

"They were just being friendly. I know a lot about science and—"

"They weren't being friendly. They were being mean. They knew you would do something like that. They're making a fool of you."

Eddy was confused. He didn't feel particularly foolish. He looked at Justin's face, even though it made him uncomfortable. Justin's eyebrows were scrunched up and the sides of his mouth were turned down, which could mean that he was mad. Why was he so mad at Eddy?

"Why do you stand for it?" continued Justin. "Is it just because Mitch is popular? All the girls say he's really good-looking."

"I do not know," said Eddy. Eddy hadn't even realized Mitch was popular. Or good-looking, for that matter. He was just Mitch. Eddy had known him forever. They went to preschool and kindergarten together. They used to play together all the time, building forts out of chairs and blankets and couch cushions. These days, Mitch was one of the few people who talked to Eddy on a regular basis.

"He's so full of himself." Justin's voice was getting

louder. "He walks around with that stupid smirk on his face, like he owns the world."

Why was Justin yelling at Eddy? Was he angry that Mitch and Eddy were friends? The conversation was getting too confusing. Tiffany would say, "When you want to change the subject, ask a question."

"Did you just move here from somewhere else this year?" asked Eddy.

"No, I've lived in Drayton all my life," replied Justin. "I just skipped a grade last year. They were thinking of having me skip two grades, but they settled for placing me in the accelerated math program. It's good because I'm not so bored, but I don't like being the youngest kid in middle school. Most of my friends are still in fifth grade. I don't get to see my old friends very much. I mean my young friends. I mean my old, younger friends."

Eddy laughed.

"I guess some of the older kids are OK," continued Justin. His glasses had slipped down his nose a bit, so he pushed them back with his finger, leaving a smear of mayonnaise on the bridge of the frame. "I mean, there's you."

This surprised Eddy, given that Justin was just yelling at him. Did Justin consider Eddy to be his friend?

"And Terry is all right," continued Justin.

"Who?"

"Terry Putnam, the audio-visual assistant."

"Oh, yes." Eddy remembered the blue hair from the science fair. Terry's hair reminded Eddy of lapis lazuli.

Technically, lapis lazuli is a rock, not a mineral, since it is made up of a mixture of minerals.

Eddy jumped with a start as a piece of paper flapped in front of his face.

"Here," said Meara. "Mr. Benton says you're supposed to pay this."

Eddy took the paper out of Meara's hand and looked at it. It was a receipt from Dry-Town Cleaners. "I do not have the money here with me today. Can I give it to you tomorrow?"

"OK," said Meara as she turned and walked away, her copper-colored curls bouncing with every step.

Fact Number 475 from the Random Access Memory of Edison Thomas: Lapis lazuli was often ground up and used as a blue pigment by Renaissance painters, including Leonardo da Vinci.

In social studies class, Eddy decided to draw a preliminary graph of his data on the traffic activity at Jim's corner. He planned to produce a computer-generated version. A bar graph was probably best. He would use a solid bar to represent the cars that entered the intersection and a hatched bar to represent cars that failed to stop at the stop sign. He could also show the traffic at different times of day. Now, how long to make the vertical axis? Should he save room for even worse days? How bad could it get?

A poke on his left shoulder blade (or scapula) interrupted

Eddy's graph making. He swung around to see who was poking him. Kip Cleghorn pointed the eraser end of his pencil toward the front of the room.

Eddy looked where Kip's pencil eraser had pointed. Mr. Adler stood with his arms crossed in front of him, tapping his right foot on the floor. "Well, Mr. Thomas, do you have an answer for us?"

"Could you repeat the question, please?" asked Eddy. That was a standard phrase in Eddy's arsenal.

"We were talking about *Common Sense* by Thomas Paine."

Eddy cleared his throat. "A long habit of not thinking a thing wrong, gives it a superficial appearance of being right, and raises at first a formidable outcry in defense of custom."

Mr. Adler consulted a book on his desk, as the hiss of whispering rose in the classroom.

"Why, yes," he said. "That's an exact quote from *Common Sense*. Excellent job, Eddy. Now if you could just tell the class what that means."

Eddy had no idea what it meant. He looked around the classroom at all the faces staring at him. He could feel his pulse rate increasing as he searched his brain for an answer.

"It, um," started Eddy. "A long habit ... of not ... thinking ..." He knew the quotation, but that was all. He was taking too long to answer the question. People were starting to whisper again. He could hear his own heart beating.

"Did you read the assignment?"

"Yes," said Eddy.

"Well, then, we are all waiting patiently for you to answer my question." Mr. Adler's voice was getting progressively louder. He didn't seem to be waiting very patiently.

Eddy didn't know what to do. The noise in his head was getting louder and louder. Finally, he bent over and banged his head on his desk. The classroom erupted with laughter.

"I'll take that as an 'I don't know,'" said Mr. Adler. "Does anyone else have any ideas?"

Adam Jackson-Delgado's hand shot up. Mr. Adler nodded at him.

"It means that people don't like change, even if it's for the better."

"Good. Anyone else?"

Eddy was glad the focus was off him. He silently recited the periodic table to calm down. *Hydrogen, helium, lithium...*

"Very good, Miss Chen," continued Mr. Adler. "Now, why did Thomas Paine support independence from Great Britain?"

... chromium, manganese, iron, cobalt ...

"He didn't think we should have a king," came a girl's voice.

... palladium, silver, cadmium ...

Eddy rolled his head around to loosen up his neck muscles and saw a water spot on the ceiling tile directly above his head. He had never noticed that before, and wondered how it got there. There might be a leak in the roof or maybe a broken pipe above the ceiling. It could have also come from below. Perhaps someone was opening a bottle of sparkling water that had been shaken up. The water could have sprayed the ceiling. Or maybe someone had made a rocket powered by vinegar (acetic acid) and baking soda (sodium bicarbonate). If the rocket hit the ceiling, then some liquid could have spilled out onto the tile. There would probably also be some damage to the tile from the nose cone hitting it. Eddy squinted to see if he could detect any tile damage near the water spot.

The slap of Eddy's Bunker Hill report hitting his desk interrupted his thoughts. The bell rang, and the room filled with the sound of sliding chairs, rustling papers, and the zipping of backpack zippers.

He looked at the report. D. Dad was going to say "I told you so."

Eddy pulled his schedule out of his right rear jeans pocket. Today was the day he would have to sit in detention after school for the ketchup incident. Eddy groaned. That meant less time working in the basement. He really needed some basement time. He folded his schedule and the stop sign graph together and stuffed them into his pocket.

On the way to detention, Eddy stopped in the library to pick up a book for his biography project.

He wandered aimlessly around the library for a while. He knew where to find the science and technology books, but he had never been to the biography section before. He located the correct row and turned left between the stacks. The pit of his stomach felt as if it dropped two feet as he looked at the biography section, which consisted of mostly empty shelves. A dozen books lay flat on four rows of shelving. He frantically picked up each one and looked at the titles. Shirley Temple. Saint Francis of Assisi. Lucretia Mott. Karl Marx. John Paul Jones. Florence Nightingale.

Why were all the interesting books gone? Was it a plot? No, he told himself. He had just waited too long to pick out a book. All the other kids had gotten there before him and checked out all the biographies of interesting people.

Donald Trump. Mary, Queen of Scots. William Penn. Lao-Tse.

Eddy felt his heart speeding up. Panic pushed at the floodgates of his brain, trying to get in. Eddy pushed back. He told himself to keep looking. One of these books had to be acceptable. The last two books were about John Quincy Adams and Maria Callas. Eddy shoved them back on the shelf.

Eddy's breathing accelerated. He knew his adrenal glands had begun putting out adrenaline, a hormone that speeds up heart rate and breathing as part of the "fight-or-flight" response. The adrenaline also increases alertness, dilates the pupils, and speeds up reflexes, all of which help improve the chances for survival in stressful situations. If some prehistoric person encountered a woolly mammoth (*Mammuthus primigenius*), he could run away to keep from getting trampled, or if he had his spear with him, he could try to kill it. Because of the fight-or-flight response, he would have been ready to do either one.

Of course, the fight-or-flight response wasn't very useful in a library, unless there were woolly mammoths in the biography section, which Eddy doubted. The best way to counteract the response he was having was to get out of the library as quickly as he could. As he turned the corner out of the stacks, he ran into a cart full of books waiting to be shelved, knocking a few of them to the floor. He looked around to see if anyone had seen his klutzy move, then stubbed his toe on a thick green book that looked as if it had been repaired a few times. He looked at the title: *Thomas Edison, The Wizard of Menlo Park.*

Eddy groaned. If he chose that book, he would never hear the end of it from Dad.

The bell rang. He was late for detention. It was Thomas Edison or nothing. He checked out the book and ran.

Fact Number 4,800,000 from the Random Access Memory of Edison Thomas: Woolly mammoths survived until about 1700 BC on the remote Wrangel Island in the Arctic Ocean, off the northern coast of Russia.

Thomas Alva Edison was born on February 11, 1847.

Eddy yawned. This book was going to make detention seem even longer.

> *The youngest of seven children, Alva (as his family called him) was always getting into trouble. His curiosity some-times ran ahead of his common sense. This resulted in many*

near misses. Once, Alva fell into a grain elevator and almost smothered. Another time, he set fire to his father's barn, the first of many accidental fires in Alva's life.

Eddy chuckled. Maybe Alva should have invented the smoke detector. He glanced around the room. Mr. Nathan was doing a crossword puzzle at his desk at the front of the room. A kid with long, stringy hair had his head on the desk by the window and was snoring loudly. A skinny girl sat in front of Eddy. The braid down her back exposed her slightly protuberant ears and big, dangly earrings that jingled, like miniature wind chimes, whenever she moved her head. Eddy didn't understand how anyone could stand to wear earrings like that. The noise would drive him crazy. As a matter of fact, the noise *was* driving him crazy. He went back to his book.

Alva was often taunted by the other children because of his unusually large head. He didn't do well in school. In fact, he only stayed in school for a few months. One teacher said he was 'addled.' His mother, Nancy, took him out of school and taught him at home. He became an insatiable reader. He enjoyed science and set up a chemistry lab in his room, which his mother insisted he move to the basement.

Miss Wind Chimes was moving her head again. Eddy wondered what she had done to deserve detention. Probably "Excessive Head Shaking."

At the age of 12, Alva went to work for the railroad, selling newspapers and snacks to the passengers. His supervisor allowed him to set up a chemistry lab in an unused corner of a baggage car. Not surprisingly, he started a fire on the train.

Maybe this guy needed to invent the portable fire extinguisher, one that you could hang from your belt or some kind of holster, like a pistol. Then he could have instant access to fire suppression in case of an unexpected incendiary event. He flipped through the rest of the chapter. More about working on the train. Eddy was impatient to find out about the invention of the light bulb. Next chapter.

At the age of 16, Alva learned to use the telegraph. The telegraph uses patterns of electrical impulses to send messages over wires. Despite his partial hearing loss, Alva was quickly able to master Morse code, where each letter is represented by a particular set of short pulses, or dots, and longer pulses, or dashes (See Appendix 1).

Eddy turned to the back of the book, where a table listed all the dots and dashes for every letter, plus numbers and punctuation marks. Morse code might be useful to him. He could send secret messages in class just by tapping them out with his pencil. But there really wasn't anyone to receive his secret messages. Mitch wasn't in any of Eddy's classes.

It didn't look too hard to learn. The easiest ones were E (•) and T (—). That was smart, since those are the two letters used most frequently in written English. They also happened to be his initials. E.T. Eddy Thomas. • — He tapped the pattern on his desk with his finger. • — • — • — ET, ET, ET.

After a few minutes, he could tap out his whole name: • (E), — • • (D), — • • (D again), — • — — (Y), — (T), • • • • (H), — — — (O), — — (M), • — (A) —

Miss Wind Chimes turned around abruptly and hissed, "Stop it, already!" Eddy jumped, stopped tapping, and then went back to reading.

Alva was fired from his first job as a telegraph operator when a chemistry experiment exploded.

Eddy suppressed a laugh.

One of his duties as a telegraph operator was to send a message every hour to make sure the line was working. Alva invented a device that would automatically send the message, allowing him to sleep uninterrupted. Since a telegraph signal only traveled 200 miles or so, telegraph operators often had to relay messages that had to travel longer distances. Alva invented an "automatic repeater" that recorded the incoming message on a strip of paper and then transmitted that same message along, eliminating the need for a human to perform the task.

Eddy's interest in Thomas Edison's inventions was piqued. Waking up every hour to send a message would cause some serious sleep deprivation, a problem with which Eddy was all too familiar. And having to relay messages could introduce human error. Sure, the light bulb was important, but these were useful, too. Eddy read about the duplex telegraph (sending two messages over the same telegraph wire), the quadruplex telegraph (sending four messages at a time), the automatic vote recorder (Edison's first patent), and the phonograph (first recorded words: "Mary had a little lamb"). Then he discovered that Appendix 2 consisted of schematic diagrams of the inventions. Maybe this book wouldn't be so bad.

After what had seemed like only a few minutes, Miss Wind Chimes jingled as she stood up and left the room. Mr. Nathan was gone as well. The stringy-haired kid was still snoring.

6. Breathe In, Breathe Out

"Mom," said Eddy with a mouthful of cornflakes. "Are there any more clean pillowcases? There are none left in the hall closet."

"I'm sorry, dear," said Mom. "I haven't had a chance to do any laundry this week." Mom worked as a freelance graphic artist. That meant that when she had a deadline, not much got done around the house. "I'll see if I can find one today while you're at school."

"Why don't you just run a load of laundry, Sarah?" suggested Dad.

"I suppose I could squeeze in the time to do that," replied Mom. "I'm hoping to get that project done today."

"How long can it take to throw some laundry in the machine and push a button?"

"I said I would try, Jeff."

"I can do it after school," offered Eddy.

"Oh, aren't you sweet! Thank you, dear." Mom gave Eddy a big hug. Although he usually hated it when people touched him, Eddy loved his mom's hugs. They squeezed him just enough to make him feel calmer.

Eddy got his schedule out to pencil in *Do Laundry* after school. He had already penciled in a note to *Learn Morse*

Code just before *Pay Dry-Cleaning Bill*. He stuck a copy of the Morse code chart he had found on the Internet into his left back pocket along with the traffic graph he had printed out the night before. He folded the dry-cleaning receipt and money together with his schedule and shoved them into his right back pocket.

"You know, you could just put those papers in your backpack," said Dad.

"But I need them with me all the time," protested Eddy.

"Are you going to memorize them by osmosis through your—"

"That's enough, Jeff," said Mom. "Eddy, you have three minutes." Eddy liked to get to school fifteen minutes early so he could avoid the last-minute crowd. The hallways were quieter and it didn't stress him out as much as when he arrived exactly on time. He had asked his mom to remind him when it was time to go. Unfortunately, Mom's reminders irritated him.

Eddy suddenly had an idea for a new invention. A talking timer. He could set it to give him gentle reminders of how much time he had left. When Mom did it, it seemed too much like nagging. A timer couldn't nag, could it? It was just an electronic device.

"Two minutes, Eddy," said Mom.

Yes, a talking timer would be an excellent invention, thought Eddy as he finished the rest of his calcium-fortified *Citrus sinensis* juice and left for school.

As soon as the intersection came into view, Eddy began monitoring the traffic at the stop sign. A red minivan came to a rolling stop. A turquoise hybrid stopped properly, but a silver sports car blew right through the intersection.

Eddy continued to tally cars as he crossed the street and as he stepped on the sidewalk, walking backward until he reached the stairs in front of the school doors and went in. He stopped at his locker, pulled the sticky note that said DWEEB off the door, and stuffed it into his backpack. He pulled the papers out of the left rear pocket of his pants and drew in more bars on his computer-generated bar graph to show the morning's traffic. Things were getting worse; of the 37 cars that reached the intersection, 24 came to a full stop and 13 did not. The picture of Lily Mae being hit by a car returned to his head. Eddy tried to get rid of the image by concentrating on something else. He looked at his Morse code chart for a while, which calmed him down a bit.

The hallway started to fill up. Eddy returned the traffic graph and Morse code chart to his left pocket and got his schedule out of the right pocket. The dry-cleaning money fell on the floor. Eddy stooped to pick it up. A dollar bill fluttered to the center of the hallway. As Eddy crawled after it, an expensive athletic shoe stepped on it, and on Eddy's fingers.

"Ouch," said Eddy, and he looked up to see Mitch's body attached to the shoe. Next to him, Mark poked his elbow into Mitch's ribs and laughed.

"There you go, E.T. We wouldn't want you to lose your money," said Mitch.

"Thank you, Mitch," said Eddy, rubbing his fingers. He was sure Mitch didn't mean to step on them. "What do you—?" But Mitch had already walked away.

Eddy gathered up the rest of the money.

"Hey, Eddy," came Justin's voice. "What did you think of the math homework? Did you get that last one? That was a killer."

"Wait," said Eddy as he finished counting the money. He had recovered it all.

"Oh, is that money for me? Thanks!"

"No, it is for Meara, to pay for dry-cleaning her sweater."

"Relax, I didn't mean it," said Justin. "Listen, do you want to go to—"

"Justin, you are in my math class!" said Eddy, pulling the papers back out of his left pocket.

"What about it?"

"I found this code we can use to communicate secretly with each other. Nobody will know what we are doing. We can tap out messages with our pencils."

"Yeah, but—"

"It is called Morse code, named after Samuel Morse, who invented it in the 1830s to use with the telegraph. They also used it for radio."

"I know what Morse code is, but I really don't—"

"Here, you can have my copy of the chart. I already memorized it." Eddy handed Justin the chart from the disorganized stack of papers in his hands.

"But—"

"I have to go find Meara to give her the money. I will see you in math class."

Eddy closed his locker and headed off to look for Meara. His head swam. All the new data on traffic at the stop sign mixed with the interactions he had already had with people that morning. Dots and dashes clicked in the background of his consciousness. He tried to focus as he rushed by students talking and locker doors opening and closing.

Finally, he spotted the back of a girl with long curly copper hair. It was Meara. She was talking to Keisha Davis. Probably about how Keisha had won first place at the science fair. Keisha was smiling, which meant she was happy. Probably not likely to drop out of the regional competition, then. Eddy realized he couldn't do anything about this year's fair.

But what about next year's fair?

Eddy could start now and come up with something amazing and, more importantly, unbeatable. His eddy coil, after all, had been a last-minute choice. It wasn't very creative. Most books with science fair projects include things like eddy coils. What he needed was something new, something nobody had done before. Maybe something to do with chaos theory. Or string theory.

"Hi, Eddy," said Keisha. Then she walked away toward the gym.

Meara turned around and looked at Eddy. She was wearing the same sweater she had been wearing on ketchup day. Eddy recognized the intricate cable pattern on the sleeves, but the ketchup was gone. That was consistent with the dry-cleaning receipt he held in his hand.

Eddy stood still.

"Yes?" asked Meara.

"Oh, I, um … Here." Eddy shoved the money toward her.

Meara took a step back and said, "Oh, thanks."

Eddy turned to go.

"Eddy?"

Eddy faced Meara.

"The dry cleaners got the stain out, see? So no hard feelings, OK?"

"Understood," said Eddy, and he headed off to class.

Fact Number 73 from the Random Access Memory of Edison Thomas: Dry cleaning is not really dry. It uses a toxic liquid called perchloroethylene. A newer, more environmentally friendly method uses supercritical carbon dioxide.

Tiffany closed the door to the office she shared with the physical therapist. Her heels clicked on the linoleum floor as she walked over to her chair. "How is your stress level today?"

"Relatively high."

"Are you still upset about not winning the science fair?"

"No, not really. I was wasting energy on something I could not do anything about. I think I will just put my energy into coming up with a better project next year."

"That's great, Eddy! I'm glad you were able to get over that. So what's bothering you now?"

"I got in trouble in the lunchroom again. And they fired Jim."

"Who's Jim?"

"The crossing guard at the corner of Delaware and Hatteras. Now the cars do not even stop at the stop sign. Well, an average of 24 percent of the cars do not come to a complete stop in the morning, and 18.4 percent do not come to a complete stop in the afternoon. I printed out a traffic graph."

Eddy pulled the graph out of his pocket and unfolded it. It was rumpled from being folded and unfolded and shoved into his pocket. Eddy carefully smoothed it out on the desk and held it down so Tiffany could appreciate it. It showed the traffic patterns at Delaware Avenue and Hatteras Street for the whole week.

Tiffany looked at it. She smoothed a few wisps of her hair with her hand. When it was pulled back tightly, as it was today, it was as black and shiny as polished onyx. "So this is stressing you out?"

"They are breaking the law, and people could get hurt."

"Maybe you should just let it go," suggested Tiffany. Eddy took his hand off the graph and the paper crinkled up a little.

Tiffany corrected herself. "I mean you should not get so stressed about it. Have you been practicing the relaxation technique I taught you?"

"Yes, but it does not work very well." Tiffany's

technique didn't work any better than reciting elements.

"What kind of picture do you make in your head?"

"I pretend I am on the rocky beach at Rock Island," said Eddy. "Not the sandy beach."

"What's Rock Island?"

"My family camps there every summer. It is very quiet because cars are not allowed on the island. I like the rocky beach, because the rocks are smooth and flat, so they are perfect for skipping across the water." Eddy proceeded to explain the physics of rock skipping. "The optimal angle for skipping rocks is 20 degrees."

"Fine, Eddy. Why don't we try some relaxation now?"

"I suppose so."

"Close your eyes and imagine you are standing on the beach at Rock Island."

"The rocky beach."

"You are standing on the rocky beach listening to the gentle waves."

"I have a box of those rocks in my room. They are mostly dolomite. That is calcium magnesium carbonate—a white or pinkish sedimentary rock. Well, it is not strictly sedimentary, because it undergoes a change after deposition through a process called diagenesis. It is not exactly metamorphic, either, but it—"

"That's great, Eddy. Let's keep working on this. I want you to take three deep breaths and let them out slowly."

As Eddy began his deep breathing, he remembered that police officers are trained to relax their bodies so that they can perform better under extremely stressful conditions. Deep rhythmic breathing can reduce levels of stress hormones, like adrenaline, circulating in the blood.

With each breath, Eddy imagined his lungs filling with oxygen. He imagined the path by which inhaled oxygen is delivered to each cell in the body.

Pulmonary vein, left atrium, left ventricle, aorta, arteries, arterioles, capillaries.

He pictured each cell taking in oxygen and releasing carbon dioxide back into the blood.

Capillaries, venules, veins, vena cava (superior and inferior), back to the heart.

Eddy pictured the heart pumping the depleted blood back to the lungs, where Eddy slowly breathed out the carbon dioxide.

"Eddy?"

"Huh?"

"Eddy, wake up," said Tiffany. "You don't want to be late for lunch."

"Yes, I mean, no, I do not want to be late." Eddy stood up and picked up his backpack.

"Good-bye, Eddy. And try to get some sleep tonight."

That was easy for Tiffany to say, thought Eddy. She probably never had nightmares.

Fact Number 28 from the Random Access Memory of Edison Thomas: Listening to slow music can lower your heart rate, while music with a faster tempo can increase your heart rate.

Eddy made it to lunch on time. He pulled his lunch out of his backpack and felt something wet—a leaky ketchup packet. Luckily, it hadn't made too much of a mess, although Eddy had no idea how it could have gotten into his backpack. As he wiped his hands with the paper napkin from his lunch, he noticed that his mother had started making those annoying drawings on his napkins again. This one was a tap dancing squirrel (*Sciurus carolinensis*) in a top hat. He crumpled it up and shoved it into his lunch bag just as Justin sat down next to him.

He was relieved that Justin had a bologna sandwich instead of *Thunnus alalunga*. The bologna smelled pretty garlicky, but Eddy didn't mind. At least it wasn't fish.

"So, Justin," said Eddy, "did you memorize the Morse code yet?"

"No," said Justin. "I wish you would stop asking me that. I really don't see the point."

"Oh, come on, it is no fun if only one person does it. Thomas Edison used it a lot. In fact, he named his first two kids *Dot* and *Dash*."

"That's just cruel," said Justin.

Eddy silently agreed. He knew what it felt like when your parents give you a stupid name. Edison Thomas was probably the stupidest name in existence, aside from Tank Engine Thomas.

"*Dot* and *Dash* were actually just nicknames," said Eddy. But still cruel, he thought.

Suddenly, someone came running up behind them and

tapped Justin on the head with a DVD case, saying, "Look! Look what I have!" Once he got over his startle reflex, Eddy recognized Terry, the AV aide with the lapis lazuli blue hair, which had faded, so that it now looked more like aquamarine.

"What is it?" asked Justin.

"It's *Tron*. The original *Tron*. My favorite movie of all time, and I get it for the whole weekend." Terry kissed the cover of the DVD, which Eddy supposed was not very sanitary. "Wanna come over and watch it with me?"

"Umm, sure," replied Justin. "Hey, Terry. This is Eddy."

Terry looked over at Eddy and said, "Hi, how are ya? So, Justin, can you come over tonight?"

"I'll have to check with my folks," said Justin. "How did you get *Tron* anyway?"

"Ms. Petronelli ordered it by accident. Her class is studying *The Iliad* by Homer, and she wanted a documentary about ancient Troy, but they sent *Tron*."

Eddy looked around to see if any teachers were nearby and whispered, "That DVD belongs to the school. You should not be taking it home."

"I do it all the time," replied Terry. "The next shipment back to the district library isn't until Monday. As long as I get it back to them in time for Monday's shipment, they're fine with it. Hey, Eddy, do you want to come and see it, too?"

Eddy didn't see any reason to go to Terry's house to watch it. "I already have a copy of it myself. It is a classic." Eddy's collection of science fiction and fantasy DVDs naturally included

Tron. Eddy didn't like the term "science fiction," because those films often included inaccurate or speculative science. He preferred to call them "fiction science." The special effects were usually good, which was why he collected these films.

"Yeah, an absolute classic," said Terry.

"What's it about?" asked Justin.

Terry explained. "This computer programmer gets inside a computer, and all the programs in the computer are people under the control of their users. They compete against each other. What makes it a classic is the way it looks. It's a milestone in computer animation."

"Actually," said Eddy, "there was not as much CGI in *Tron* as most people think."

"CGI?" asked Justin.

"Computer generated imagery," replied Eddy. "A lot of the look of *Tron* was achieved by backlit animation, where black-and-white live-action film was colorized and rotoscoped to make it look as if the action is taking place inside a computer." Eddy liked to figure out how the special effects worked in fantasy and fiction science films. Then he could find out if he was right by watching the special features on the DVD or looking it up on the Internet.

"It's kind of fun to watch now, because it was all so futuristic at the time," said Terry.

"When was it made?" asked Justin.

"Sometime in the eighties," said Terry, looking at the DVD case to find the exact date.

Eddy knew. "1982. Steven Lisberger directed it."

"When you look at it now, everything looks so primitive and clunky," said Terry. "But it was way ahead of its time."

"Yes, it was amazingly prescient," added Eddy.

"Precious?" asked Justin.

"Prescient," corrected Eddy.

"What does that mean?" asked Justin.

"It means it predicted a lot of the technology we have now, like computer-generated language and language recognition, the Internet, artificial intelligence, and computer viruses."

"Yeah," said Terry. "Some people even say that *Tron* was the inspiration for the *Matrix* trilogy, what with the whole idea of living in a virtual reality controlled by a computer."

"*The Matrix* was released in 1999 and directed by Andy and Larry Wachowski," added Eddy. "*The Matrix Reloaded* and *The Matrix Revolutions* were both released in 2003, and they were also directed by the Wachowskis."

"That's more than I wanted to know," said Justin.

"Are you sure you don't want to watch it with us, Eddy?" asked Terry.

"I am sure," said Eddy. "I will just watch my copy."

"Suit yourself," said Terry. "I gotta go. Call me after you talk to your folks, Justin."

After Terry left, Eddy and Justin ate their lunches quietly. Eddy liked it when they just ate their lunches without talking. It let him concentrate on the task at hand and he stood a chance of actually finishing his lunch. After a while, Justin asked Eddy, "Why don't you want to watch the movie with us?"

"I told you," said Eddy. "I have a copy I can watch any-time at my house."

"It might be fun to watch it together," said Justin. "Don't you like Terry?"

"He seems like a nice guy."

Justin choked on his milk and began to cough. Eddy ran through the Heimlich maneuver in his head. If someone is choking, you are supposed to grab him from behind. Make a fist, wrap your other hand around the fist, and place your hands between the navel and the ribcage. Thrust up into the diaphragm repeatedly until the object is expelled from the airway. But if the patient is coughing or able to talk, that means he can still get air and you shouldn't do the Heimlich.

Justin wasn't coughing anymore—he was laughing.

"What is the matter?" asked Eddy.

Now Justin couldn't stop laughing. Why? Was he laughing at Eddy?

"What?" said Eddy. "Did I say something funny?"

Justin finally calmed down enough to talk. He wiped a tear from his eye (Was he crying now?) and said, "Terry's a girl!"

7. Brain Storm

By the time Eddy finished erasing, the only thing left on the end of his pencil was the metal band that had held the eraser in place; it had been chewed into an irregular, vaguely starlike shape. Tiffany had suggested he write a letter to the editor of *The Drayton Times* about Jim and the stop sign. She said if he actually did something about his problem, it would make him less stressed about it.

The blood of innocent children will be on your hands.

No.

The people at City Hall must have mothballs instead of brains.

No.

Do you morons think a simple stop sign is enough to protect these kids?

No.

I have calculated that at the current rate of cars ignoring that stop sign, the probability of a fatal or near-fatal accident within the next two months is ...

No.

Eddy wondered if they would publish his graph if he sent it along with the letter. Writing was definitely not his strong point. Tiffany had also suggested that he write up a petition and get a lot of people to sign it. Again, not one of his strong points. What was his strong point?

Inventions. He could invent something that would make the intersection safer. Something that would make people stop at that stop sign. That would be a much better project to occupy his time (and brain) than some theoretical project for next year's science fair. He would actually be helping people, maybe even saving lives. That was better than a blue ribbon or even a plaque from the regional fair. He began to sketch out some ideas for traffic-calming devices.

His first idea was a robotic Jim. He could construct a robot that would wheel itself into the middle of the intersection whenever a child needed to cross the street. It could hold up a stop sign and, once the child had crossed the street, wheel itself back onto the sidewalk. If a car ran the stop sign and hit the robot, he could just make another one. At least it wouldn't be like his dream about Jim. No, robotics would be too expensive. Eddy tried to erase his drawing, but he had no eraser left on his pencil. He scribbled it out and turned the page.

He could make a crossing gate like the ones at railroad crossings. The child wishing to cross could push a button to lower the gate as lights flashed and bells clanged. No, too big and too noisy. He scribbled over that drawing.

Mom brought over a glass of milk and a plate of chocolate chip cookies with walnuts (*Juglans regia*). She must have finished her latest work project. Whenever she was between assignments, she did all sorts of homemaker-type things: baking cookies, cleaning the oven, planting shrubs, reorganizing the closets. She looked over his shoulder at the somewhat confused sketches in his notebook. "Not going well, huh?" she said.

Eddy growled with a mouth full of cookie.

"It looks as if you're getting stuck in the details again," she said. "Why don't you try just loosening your brain up a little? Do some brainstorming."

Eddy growled again as he took a sip of milk.

"Fine, fine," said Mom, stepping away. "I can take a hint. Just bring the glass and plate to the sink when you're done, please."

Eddy turned to a fresh page. He slid his hand down the smooth paper. He took a deep breath, closed his eyes, and rolled his head back. Brainstorming. That was a strange word. A storm in one's brain. Eddy knew what that was like.

It was like the science fair, when the feedback from the sound system had set off a storm in his brain. The onset of a brain storm felt like the onset of a thunderstorm, with its heavy downpours and violent, gusting winds, only the cloudburst occurred in his head. Eddy usually tried to hold back the storm, but sometimes it felt like trying to swim up Niagara Falls. When it got really bad, all he could do was ride it out and try to survive. He would squat, pulling himself into as tight a ball as he could, and stare at the floor, reciting elements until it blew over.

Eddy had learned to avoid situations where a brain storm might be imminent. Crowded events were usually a problem, especially when accompanied by loud music. Or balloons. Eddy despised balloons. They had a habit of popping and making huge, loud, sudden, startling noises. To Eddy, the tension produced by noise and lights and crowds reminded him of the gathering clouds of an approaching storm.

Dogs can always tell when a storm is approaching. Do they hear distant thunder that humans can't hear? Dogs do have hearing that is more acute than human hearing, and the range of frequencies they can detect is much wider. Eddy sometimes felt as if his own hearing was more acute than other people's, since sounds that other people didn't even appear to notice were irritating, or even unbearable, to him.

People can sense approaching storms, too. Eddy's grandpa (Becket Thomas) always claimed to know when a storm was coming because his "rheumatism" would act up. It could be because of the drop in barometric pressure, but Eddy wasn't sure. Justin probably knew all about that. His second-prize-winning, trip-to-regionals-earning tornado poster had something about barometric pressure.

Eddy shook his head, trying to dislodge the image of "brain storms" from his consciousness. He looked down at his notebook. The page in front of him was covered with scribbles so intense they tore through the paper in spots. This was getting him nowhere near solving the traffic problem at Jim's corner.

Eddy finished his cookies and milk and brought the glass and plate into the kitchen. He decided to take a break and read more about Thomas Edison. He looked in his backpack, but the book wasn't there. A little spurt of panic began to leak into his brain, but he plugged it up. *It has to be here somewhere. Ask Mom, the finder of all lost things.* First, he had to find Mom.

"MOM!"

"I'm right here," came Mom's voice, faintly, from the living room.

"Where is my book?" yelled Eddy.

"Come here and ask me."

Eddy went to the living room and stood in the arched doorway. He raised his arms to a horizontal position, pressing his hands against both sides of the opening. If he pushed hard enough, maybe he could support his weight. He tried to lift his feet. This was harder than he thought.

"Yes?" said Mom.

"Have you seen my book about Thomas Edison?" asked Eddy. Mom was knitting. Yes, she was definitely finished with her latest assignment.

"Inside voice, please," said Mom quietly. "I think I saw it in the upstairs bathroom."

Eddy liked to watch Mom knit. The rhythm was calming. *Click, click,* flip the yarn, *click, click,* flip. It looked like yet another scarf, about twenty centimeters wide. Eddy suddenly realized that knitting could be the basis of a secret code. You could knit a rectangle, and then write your message on it. Then you unravel it and send the ball of yarn to the recipient, who would then re-knit the rectangle and read the message. Only someone who knew the exact dimensions of the rectangle and the right size needles to use would be able to regenerate the message. If you used water-soluble ink to write the message, you could plunge the rectangle into water to erase the message once you'd read it. It reminded Eddy of those old movies in which the spies eat the paper with the secret message to keep it from falling into enemy hands. That couldn't be good for you. Eddy wondered what the nutritive value of paper could be.

"Eddy," said Mom.

"Yes."

"Upstairs bathroom. Thomas Edison."

"Right, thank you."

"You're welcome."

Eddy bounded up the stairs to the bathroom. Sure enough, the book was on the floor. Eddy picked it up, carried it to his room, and flopped down on the bed.

He opened it to where he had left off. Page 83.

In his lifetime, Edison obtained over 1,000 patents. Once, when he was asked about the secret to his prodigious output, he replied, "To invent, you need a good imagination and a pile of junk."

"Of course!" Eddy said out loud. He had been trying to invent on paper, when he needed to be getting ideas from his own pile of junk in the basement. He dropped the book, making a mental note to remember where—on his bed—and went to the basement.

Along one wall, Eddy had carefully organized and cataloged a collection of parts salvaged from junk he had found and things that Dad had brought home from work—drawers and drawers full of transistors, thermocouples, light-emitting diodes, gears, motors, switches, capacitors, timer motors, relays, and circuit boards. He had piled the stuff he hadn't gotten around to disassembling against the far wall. His pile of junk. He stood motionless and stared at it, waiting for inspiration, just like Thomas Edison.

Nothing happened.

He gave the pile a forceful kick. Still nothing, except a sore toe. He had neglected to put some shoes on his feet.

Another kick, this one a little more careful. A metal detector fell from the top of the pile and landed with a crash at Eddy's (shoeless) feet. Eddy picked it up and examined it. It didn't seem to have been damaged in the fall.

A metal detector. Cars are made of metal. A transmitter coil creates a magnetic field. If the magnetic field interacts with a piece of metal, that piece of metal generates its own magnetic field, which is picked up by the receiver coil. He could set up a metal detector near the stop sign and … no. He would not be able to tell if the car had stopped moving.

Eddy kept looking. A TV remote. A waffle iron. A fax machine. A toy computer that talked when you pushed the buttons. Eddy stopped to think. The voice synthesizer in the toy computer might be useful for the talking timer he was planning to invent.

Back to business. An old telephone with a rotary dial. An eight-track tape player. A singing fish. A lamp. A calculator. A barometer.

Eddy stopped, dropped the barometer (cracking the glass cover), and picked up the singing fish. It was one of those gag gifts that looks like a regular trophy fish, in this case, a large-mouth bass (*Micropterus salmoides salmoides*). If someone walked by, it would start singing some dumb song. The key was that it *sensed* if someone was walking by. Eddy took the fish to his workbench and took it apart. Sure enough, inside was a photoreceptor. But would it work on his invention? It seemed like a simple photoreceptor that would just detect whether something was directly in front of it. What he really needed was something that would tell him if a car stops or is still moving. He dropped the fish and went back to his junk pile. This time he was searching for something in particular.

He started digging, looking for the motion-activated light fixture he had picked up a few months ago. The motion detector on the light fixture would be much more sensitive to the subtle difference between a rolling stop and a full stop. As he was searching, he picked up a remote control from an automatic garage door opener and got another idea. Modern automatic garage door openers have infrared safety devices. These send out an infrared beam that stops the garage door from closing if something breaks the beam. He could use that, too. He spent the rest of the afternoon collecting the components and assembling his prototype invention, thanks to Thomas Alva Edison and his useful advice.

8. Dead (or at Least Mortally Wounded) End

When his Wake-Upper kicked in, Eddy woke up feeling relaxed and rested. He had had his first full night of sleep in weeks. Not a single nightmare. He had been dreaming about solutions to the traffic problem instead of its disastrous consequences. Eddy left early, hoping to install his prototype traffic monitor before school. His design would work in theory, but he needed to test it in the real world in case he had overlooked any variables. What works in the basement may not work on two tons of steel.

He measured ten meters from the stop sign and set up the infrared light and detector he had scavenged from the garage door opener's safety device. On the other side of the street, he set up a reflector and carefully aligned it so that it would reflect the infrared beam back at the detector. Cars that broke the beam of infrared light would be counted as cars approaching the intersection. A wire connected the infrared detector to the motion detector and master control unit, which he placed next to the stop sign. Once a car broke the infrared beam, the motion detector would determine if cars approaching the intersection came to a full stop at the stop sign.

He wanted to test his monitor both in the morning

and in the afternoon, since his data indicated that more cars fail to come to a complete stop in the morning than in the afternoon. He also didn't want to be late for school, so he checked his watch every minute. He had set his watch alarm to go off ten minutes before school began, but he kept checking, just in case. He supposed he would be able to tell that school was about to start because of the number of students approaching the school, but he didn't trust himself to notice if he was engrossed in his invention.

To fine-tune his monitor, he had to wait for cars to come through the intersection. He had replaced the capacitor in the motion-activated light fixture with a smaller one. If he had left the original, larger capacitor in, cars would have to hold still for ten seconds to keep from triggering the motion detector. That was not likely to happen. With the new capacitor, he had gotten the time down to one second.

Eddy watched and recorded cars in the intersection for a while. After about twenty minutes, he made some calculations and compared the results with his graph of data from the previous weeks. He was surprised to find that the percentage of cars that ran the stop sign was much lower that morning than on any of the other mornings he had observed. What were the chances of that?

Maybe the blinders on the motion detector needed to be adjusted. The blinders allow the motion detector to detect the motion of cars in the intersection without detecting other motions in the immediate area, like the large man who walked by with a *Canis familiaris* (breed: Irish wolfhound).

Eddy adjusted the blinders a little and watched some more. Every time a car came through the intersection, he checked the counters on the monitor. He had gotten the counters from old commercial washing machines. One counter (connected to the infrared garage door safety device) counted cars entering the intersection. The second counter (connected to the motion detector) counted cars that failed to stop for at least one second. The counters seemed to be recording the events correctly. So why were things different today?

"Hey, E.T.!" A forceful slap on the back almost knocked Eddy over.

Eddy looked up to see Mitch and his buddy Mark.

"Oh, hi!" replied Eddy. "Do you want to see what I ..."

But Mitch and Mark were already waddling away like penguins (genus *Aptenodytes*).

Eddy was still confused about the difference between his old data and his new data, so he continued to fiddle with the monitor, even after the alarm on his watch beeped. Within the time he had been observing that morning, significantly fewer cars blew through the stop sign than he had recorded on his bar graph from previous observations. Was the invention working already? But how? It was only recording events. Eddy hadn't even begun to work on the problem of how to signal that a car had ignored the stop sign.

Suddenly, Eddy heard a roar and coughed, inhaling diesel exhaust as a school bus accelerated out of the intersection. School was about to start. Eddy hastily reset the counters and closed the access panel on the monitor, screwing it into place with a quarter-inch nut driver, which he then shoved into his backpack.

Eddy rushed into school and bolted up the steps to his locker. He pulled the sticky note that said WEIRDO off his locker door and tried unsuccessfully to sneak quietly into homeroom.

The discrepancy between the way cars (or, more accurately, their drivers) seemed to act when the monitor was in place and how they had acted in the past dominated Eddy's thoughts throughout the school day. Eddy went out to his monitor when lunch period started to see what had been recorded during the morning. The data got more confusing. The numbers on the counters were pretty much the same as the numbers on his graph, the numbers he had recorded before this morning, not like the strange numbers he had gotten before school.

He decided to watch the intersection for the entire lunch period. Over lunch, the numbers of cars running the stop sign were very low again, as they had been in the morning. He continued to think about the problem for the rest of the afternoon.

The first thing Eddy did when he left school that afternoon was to eat his peanut butter and bee vomit sandwich. His stomach had been growling all afternoon because he had neglected to bring his lunch out with him when he observed his monitor during lunch period. He hadn't had time to eat anything during the rest of the day.

When he reached the corner, he noticed that the top of the monitor was wet. This puzzled Eddy, because it hadn't rained. He touched the puddle on the monitor and smelled his finger. Urine. Disgusted, Eddy wiped his hands vigorously on the grass, then on his pants. Apparently, a dog (*Canis familiaris*) had mistaken his monitor for a fire hydrant. More likely, the dog had noticed a new object in its territory and marked it as its own. He unzipped his backpack to get his quarter-inch nut driver and opened the access panel. The inside of the monitor was dry. Eddy was relieved that it was protected from the pee and confident that it would be safe from rain as well.

Eddy began checking the settings in his monitor. He looked up briefly and noticed someone loitering across the street. Was he being watched? He shrugged and got a piece of paper and a pencil from his backpack.

"Whoops!" Mitch's voice startled Eddy, and when he looked up, he saw his quarter-inch nut driver skittering down the sidewalk and rolling off the curb. Then he noticed Mitch and Will standing over him.

"Hey, E.T., you should be careful where you leave your screwdrivers," said Will.

"Actually, it is a quarter-inch nut driver," said Eddy as he scrambled to his feet and stumbled over to pick it up before it went down the storm sewer.

Will and Mitch howled with laughter. Eddy didn't say anything as he put the nut driver into his backpack. He shouldn't have left it in the middle of the sidewalk. He could have tripped someone.

The laughter diminished as Mitch and Will walked away. Suddenly Mitch stopped. "Hey, Eddy!"

"What?"

"Phone home!"

Will and Mitch laughed even harder. Eddy wondered what he meant by that. Did Mitch know something Eddy didn't? Eddy didn't have a cell phone with him, so he filed Mitch's comment in the back of his brain and continued working on the monitor.

As the loiterer crossed the street, Eddy recognized Kip Cleghorn from social studies class. Kip was the only boy he knew who wore his hair in a ponytail. As he walked toward Eddy, his big toes popped in and out of holes in his black high-top sneakers.

"Hi, Eddy," said Kip.

"Hi," said Eddy. He wondered if Kip was going to want to have a conversation. Tiffany had said that a good way to start a conversation is by talking about something you have in common with the other person or something that interests you both. Eddy looked at Kip's T-shirt. It had some writing on it: *AC/DC.*

"Are you interested in electricity?" Eddy asked.

"Only when it powers my guitar."

"Can your guitar run on both alternating and direct current?"

"What does that mean?"

"Do you plug it into an outlet on the wall, or can you run it off a battery pack or plug it into the cigarette lighter in a car?"

"I plug it into the wall, but it would be great to use a battery pack. Then I could play anywhere, even in the middle of a field or on the beach. My mom sometimes complains when I practice at home."

"Then your T-shirt should just say *AC*, because you do not at this time have the capacity to run your guitar on direct current."

"What?"

"AC/DC would mean you can use both sources of power," said Eddy, pointing at Kip's shirt.

"Oh! I get it. That's a good one," laughed Kip. "*AC/DC* is the name of a heavy metal band".

Eddy listed the heavy metals in his head. Some, such as cobalt, copper, iron, manganese, molybdenum, vanadium, strontium, and zinc, are needed by the body in trace amounts, but excessive levels can be detrimental. Other heavy metals such as mercury, lead, and cadmium have no beneficial effects and are toxic.

"A rock band," continued Kip.

Sedimentary, igneous, metamorphic.

"You know, music."

"I like They Might Be Giants," said Eddy. "I like that they use science in their lyrics and that the science is accurate. I hate it when people get the science wrong."

"I like They Might Be Giants, too. What's your favorite song?"

"It is called 'Mammal.' It is the only song in the world, to my knowledge, with the word *monotreme* in its lyrics."

"What's a monotreme?"

"Monotremes are mammals that lay eggs."

"Mammals don't lay eggs."

"Monotremes do. The duck-billed platypus and the spiny anteater, also known as the echidna, are monotremes. They are unique, which is what I like about them." Eddy resisted the urge to recite the Latin names of the duck-billed platypus (*Ornithorhynchus anatinus*) and the echidna (family Tachyglossidae). Tiffany said some people think it is strange to use Latin names for everything.

"I like 'Birdhouse in Your Soul' and 'Istanbul (Not Constantinople)' from *Flood*."

"I like that CD, too."

"I'll bet you also like 'Why Does The Sun Shine' otherwise known as 'The Sun is a Mass of Incandescent Gas'. That has a lot of science, too."

"It is a catchy song, but the science is no longer accurate. Since that song was written in the 1950s, scientists have established that the sun is made of plasma, not gas."

"Then They Might Be Giants didn't write it?"

"No, but they made a new song to reflect new scientific findings. It is on the *Here Comes Science* CD released in 2009. The new song is called 'Why Does the Sun Really Shine?' or 'The Sun Is a Miasma of Incandescent Plasma.' I prefer the newer, more accurate version."

"Why am I not surprised?" Kip laughed.

"I do not know," said Eddy. Kip seemed to be asking him to read his mind, just as Dad did.

"You know, I've been trying to get my band to play some They Might Be Giants songs, but they say they're too geeky."

"I prefer the term *quirky*."

"Well, they're too quirky for my band."

"I think you should play them. What is your band called?"

"Western Blot."

Eddy gave a hearty laugh. "Why did you name your band after a protein analysis technique?"

"A what?"

"Western blot is a way to analyze proteins in the laboratory. First you separate the proteins by molecular weight using an electric current, and then you transfer the proteins onto a membrane and use antibodies to—"

"Obviously, we had no idea what it meant. I think Trevor just picked it out of a newspaper. The other guys want to change it because they say it makes us sound like we play country music, which we don't. I like it, though. It sounds angry and political."

"Oh no, I forgot," said Eddy suddenly. "Do you have a cell phone?"

"No, why?"

"For some reason, Mitch says I need to phone home."

"You think he's serious?" asked Kip.

"Yes," said Eddy. "Why not?"

"He's just trying to get your goat."

Eddy laughed. "I do not have a goat (genus *Capra*), but I

do have a rabbit. Her name is *Orycto* … umm … O.C." Maybe people wouldn't think it was strange to use the *initials* of the Latin name.

"Yeah, well, I think Mitch is calling you an alien, an extraterrestrial. You know, 'E.T. phone home.'"

Eddy remembered now. *E.T.: The Extra-Terrestrial* was a movie released in 1982 and directed by Steven Spielberg. Eddy had the DVD of *E.T.: The Extra-Terrestrial* in his fiction science collection—the Twentieth Anniversary Edition, released in 2002. The plot involved an alien who got stranded on Earth and became friends with some kids. Eddy thought the contraption E.T. built to "phone home" was silly. It was made of things like a circular saw blade, an umbrella, and aluminum foil. Such a device could never actually broadcast a message into space. The special effects were OK in the original version, but they were better in the re-release. They even used digital technology to replace the guns the police were holding with walkie-talkies.

Why hadn't he made the connection between Mitch's comment and the movie?

"Why would Mitch call me an alien?" he asked Kip. "We have known each other since we were little kids."

"Well, you sometimes do things that are kind of … unusual," said Kip.

"Like what?"

"You talk sort of like a robot."

"So?"

"And you have a weird way of walking. Almost like you're walking on tiptoe."

"But *E* and *T* are my initials, for *Eddy Thomas*. Mitch just addresses me by my initials."

"What is *Eddy* short for, *Edward* or *Edmund* or what?"

Eddy didn't want to tell Kip his real name, because he might make fun of it. Then again, he might be OK with it. "*Edison*. That was my dad's idea. It is a really stupid family tradition."

"I know about stupid family traditions. My real name isn't *Kip*. It's *Howard*, after my grandfather, but I refuse to answer to that. So what are you working on? Another science fair project?"

A science fair project? Maybe. It would certainly be easier than a demonstration of string theory.

"It is a device for detecting when people run the stop sign. When a car or truck breaks the infrared light beam, the motion detector will be activated and will determine if the vehicle is moving. If the vehicle stops before it crosses the plane of the stop sign for at least one second, it will not do anything, but if it fails to stop, some kind of alarm will go off. I have not quite figured out the alarm system yet."

"So the alarm system sounds if the car runs the stop sign."

"Yes, because by law you are supposed to come to a complete stop at a stop sign."

"The alarm goes off after they've broken the law."

"Correct."

"What good does that do?"

"Well they broke the law, so—"

"Does it help the pedestrians?"

"Of course, because the cars need to stop, so they can cross safely."

"But by the time the alarm sounds, the car could have hit the pedestrian."

Eddy pictured this. Then he pictured himself running into a brick wall. How could he have been so stupid? He had made a huge logical error. As big as Uluru/Ayers rock (346 meters high). No, even bigger. As big as the Rock of Gibraltar (426 meters high). And he didn't see it. He was so focused on the rule that he had ignored the reason for the rule.

He crossed the street to pick up the reflector, then returned to collect the infrared light detector and wound up the connecting wire as he walked back toward the stop sign. He picked up the control unit and used his sleeve to wipe the dog pee off it, fighting the nausea that was rising in his throat. With the books already in his backpack, he couldn't fit the meter in, so he put his backpack on and carried the meter home in his arms, slinging the coil of connecting wire over his shoulder.

After he had walked thirty meters, he heard Kip's voice.

"So I'll see you tomorrow then, Eddy?"

Eddy didn't say anything in reply but continued home and went straight to the basement.

Fact Number 1.7 from the Random Access Memory of Edison Thomas: The male duck-billed platypus (*Ornithorhynchus anatinus*) has poisonous spurs on its ankles.

9. KISS Me, You Fool

Eddy's traffic nightmares returned, and once again they included Jim, or rather, Jims. Multiple copies of Jim paced mechanically back and forth across the street, only to be picked off, one by one, like ducks in an old-time arcade shooting gallery.

He decided that the best way to stop the nightmares was to fix the problem with his invention. He went back to the drawing board or, more precisely, the junk pile. Kip's observation haunted him. His whole strategy for detecting whether cars stop at the stop sign wouldn't do any good for the pedestrians. He needed something that would predict if the cars were going to stop, and alert the pedestrians ahead of time, to avoid being hit. That seemed impossible. How was he going to predict the future? Was there a crystal ball in his pile of junk?

He rummaged around a bit. A hand-held video game. A weed whacker. A vacuum cleaner.

He thought some more. Drivers who have no intention of stopping would probably be going faster than those who intended to stop. In fact, Eddy had noticed that correlation while he was testing the old, failed version of the monitor.

But how could he measure velocity? He wished he had

a radar gun in his junk pile, like the police use to catch speeders. Radar guns bounce radio waves off an object to determine how fast it is moving. Eddy probably couldn't get his hands on a radar gun, so he would need to build one himself. Unless he did some careful shielding, the microwave-range radio waves could be dangerous.

Then there was lidar, which works on the same principle, but uses pulses of light from a laser. Sometimes the police use lidar, and they can take a picture of the offending vehicle. That would be good, thought Eddy. Catch them in the act. But lidar could also be dangerous. Eddy imagined a six-year-old looking directly into the laser. It would not be pretty.

He could also use ultrasound waves. Some cameras use pulses of ultrasonic waves to measure distance, like bats and dolphins use echolocation or sonar. That would be really complicated, too. Panic was starting to leak into Eddy's head. He'd never get this figured out, and somebody could get hurt.

Dad came into the basement. "Having trouble?" he asked.

"How can you tell?"

"Well, you sort of start to vibrate when your thoughts are getting out of control. What's the problem?"

"I need to determine the speed of cars at the stop sign, but I am having trouble coming up with a design for a radar gun."

"A radar gun? That would be complicated. Let me tell

you about something my uncle Sawyer taught me when I was young. It's called the KISS principle."

"Gross, Dad."

"It has nothing to do with smooching," Dad assured him. "K-I-S-S stands for Keep It Simple, Stupid. You're overthinking the problem."

"What do you mean?"

"What is speed?"

"Velocity."

"It's the distance traveled per unit of time. You don't really need to measure velocity. All you need to do is measure distance and time."

A small point of clarity began to grow in Eddy's cluttered head. Distance. Time. "I do not need to measure the speed of the cars the whole time, just the time it takes to travel between two points. That would give me the velocity."

"Exactly."

The clear spot in Eddy's head expanded. He just had to break the problem down into simpler parts. Sometimes Dad had good ideas, although Eddy would never admit it. Now, how would he detect the car?

"Eddy … EDDY," said his dad.

"Yes."

"It's time for bed. You have school tomorrow."

"I know."

Dad had begun opening and closing the drawers of his workbench. "Now, where did I put my needle-nose pliers?"

Again, Dad was asking him to read his mind.

Fact Number 20 from the Random Access Memory of Edison Thomas: African elephants (*Loxodonta africana*) can communicate over long distances by making sounds that have a frequency below the range of human hearing.

On the way to school the next day, Eddy stopped at the intersection of Hatteras and Delaware to ponder his latest puzzle. He still didn't know how to detect the position of a car to determine its velocity. He closed his eyes, inhaled, and tried to imagine he was on the beach. It was no use. How could he pretend he was at Rock Island when he kept hearing cars? There are no cars on Rock Island.

He stood on the sidewalk and watched the cars pass in front of him. Twenty-one cars went by, but only sixteen came to a complete stop. He looked at the cars and thought about radio waves, sound waves, and laser beams bouncing off the sides of the car. A metal detector might work, but Eddy wasn't sure the distance between the curb and the car would be small enough for a detector to be effective.

Eddy jumped at the loud crunching sound as the tire of a car flattened an aluminum can. A light bulb turned on in his head. (Ever since he had seen a cartoon character get an idea by having a picture of a light bulb appear over his head, Eddy often saw that very same light bulb turn on in his head when he got a sudden great idea.)

Eddy had been thinking of electronic detection devices that would sense the presence of a car through the air. A simpler idea would be to use the weight of the car, to design something that would sense when the car ran over it.

Excited by his revelation, Eddy hurried along to school. When he got there, he removed the sticky note that said DORK from his locker door and discovered that the door was jammed. Once he managed to open the door, he saw the reason for the jam. It was jam. And ketchup. And mustard. And mayonnaise. The locker had been completely filled with condiment packets, which spilled onto the floor at his feet. He looked around to see if anyone had witnessed this condiment event, but luckily the hall was empty this early in the day.

Eddy didn't want to spend another afternoon in detention, so he hurriedly picked up the packets and began shoving them into his backpack. His heart rate increased as his fight-or-flight response kicked in. He tried to fit all the packets into his backpack before students started to show up. Several of the packets had leaked, covering his history book with a pink mixture of ketchup and fat-free ranch dressing. He wiped the book clean with his sleeve.

… *zinc, gallium, germanium, arsenic, selenium* …

Eddy let out an audible squeak as someone tapped him on the shoulder.

"What did you do?" asked Justin.

Eddy exhaled forcefully. "I did not do anything. Somebody filled my locker with these things. They must have slid them through the ventilation slots. That is probably why some of them are broken. They must have been torn as they went through."

"I'll give you three guesses who did it, and the first two don't count."

"What?"

"Who do you think did it?"

"I do not know. Meara, maybe. She might be getting me back for wrecking her sweater."

"She told you she wasn't mad, didn't she?" said Justin. "Come on, it's obvious."

"Who?"

"Mitch, that's who." Justin's voice was getting louder.

"Why would he do something like this? Maybe he wanted me to have enough ketchup to test his ketchup gun. But you said he did not really want me to make him a ketchup gun."

"He's trying to get you in trouble again. Mitch isn't your friend, Eddy. He makes fun of you and trips you and pushes you around."

Eddy didn't say anything as he shoved the rest of the packets into his locker. Eddy wished Justin was wrong, but what if he were right? What if all those friendly slaps on the back weren't so friendly? Mitch and Eddy used to build forts together and pretend they were working together to defend themselves against the evil attackers. Mitch-Man and Super-Eddy saved the world from giant robotic lobsters (*Homarus americanus*) and mutant garbage cans. Could Mitch-Man have gone to the other side?

"See you later," said Justin.

Eddy looked at his stained sleeve. He hoped he would be able to tolerate the smell of ketchup and ranch dressing all day.

Fact Number 44 from the Random Access Memory of Edison Thomas: Lobsters (family Nephropidae) can be green, blue, yellow, red, or white. All lobsters (except white albino lobsters) turn red when cooked. Lobster blood is clear and colorless. When exposed to oxygen, it turns blue.

"We're going to work on some stories today," said Tiffany, pulling six big cards from an envelope and spreading them out on the table. Each card had a different picture on it. "I'd like you to arrange these cards so that they tell a story," she explained. "Then we'll talk about the story."

Eddy jumped when Tiffany's beeper beeped. Tiffany looked at the beeper and said, "I'll just be a minute." Eddy watched her walk out of the room, her ankles teetering precariously on top of her shoes. How did people stay upright on heels that high? It seemed to defy the laws of physics.

Eddy picked up a card to look at it a little closer. Just a black-and-white drawing of some people. He turned the card over. No picture, but it said *Social Cue Cards, Set 15. Copyright Educational Access, Inc.* At the bottom, Eddy saw a small number 3. He turned over another card: *Social Cue Cards, Set 15. Copyright Educational Access, Inc.* This one had a number 2 at the bottom. He turned the rest of the cards over. They all had different numbers on them. He arranged the cards on the table so the numbers were in order and then turned them back over so the pictures were up.

He had been working long enough with Tiffany to know that she would ask him to tell her a story based on the expressions on the kids' faces. Before she came back into the room, he could get a head start analyzing the facial features. He looked at the first card. A tall boy in a group of kids was pointing a finger at a girl who was standing to the side. Why was he pointing? Was he choosing her for his team?

Eddy looked closer. The big kid's nose was crunched up. He looked as if he had just eaten a very sour apple (*Malus domestica*), maybe one with a worm in it, like an apple maggot (*Rhagoletis pomonella*). Or half an apple maggot. That would be worse. Or maybe he thought the girl smelled bad.

Mitch sometimes had that sour-apple look on his face when he talked to Eddy. What did that mean? Did he think Eddy smelled funny?

Sometimes, Mitch smiled and laughed. Eddy had always thought that a smile meant somebody was happy. And a laugh meant something was funny. Was Mitch making fun of Eddy? Was he happy about it?

But Justin laughed and smiled at Eddy, too. Was Justin making fun of Eddy? Eddy wished people weren't so hard to figure out.

The next card (card 2) showed the girl with her hands over her face. How was he supposed to analyze the expression on her face if he couldn't see it?

Card 3 showed the girl turning away from the group and the rest of the group turning toward the tall kid. The kids weren't smiling at the tall boy. Instead, the ends of their mouths were pointing down and their eyebrows were squeezed together. Just like Justin when he talked about Mitch. Maybe Justin was mad at Mitch and not at Eddy, because Justin thought Mitch was making fun of Eddy. So is it OK for friends to get mad?

Tiffany wobbled back into the room, wheeled a chair over from her desk, and sat down next to Eddy. "Sorry that took so long," she said. "How did you do?"

"Pretty well, I think," replied Eddy.

"Let's have a look," said Tiffany. She examined the cards and looked at Eddy's face. One corner of her mouth turned up, like half a smile. "Now tell me about the story."

Eddy could feel the adrenaline in his body increase. He wondered if Tiffany knew that he'd cheated. He hadn't had time to complete his facial analysis, other than the sour-apple look and the mad thing.

Why did it take him so long to figure these things out? Justin seemed to be quicker about it. He was probably a lot better at it, too. Was Justin right about Mitch not being Eddy's friend? He and Mitch used to be best buddies. When did that change?

Eddy heaved a huge sigh.

"Eddy, is something wrong?"

Eddy didn't want to say it, because if he said it, it would be true. He asked a question instead. "How can I tell if someone is being mean to me?"

"Has someone been hurting you?"

"No, nobody has hit me or anything." Although Mitch sometimes pushed him real hard.

Tiffany stared at Eddy for an uncomfortably long period of time. "Have you told Mr. Benton about this?"

"No."

"Maybe you should."

Eddy shrugged. He didn't see what good it would do to tell the principal about his inability to figure out who his friends were. He would probably get another detention. For cluelessness.

Tiffany wheeled across the room in her chair to a file cabinet. That was a good strategy to prevent spraining an ankle in those shoes, thought Eddy. She opened the bottom drawer, got out a pamphlet, and wheeled back over to Eddy. "You might want to read this."

Eddy glanced at the pamphlet. *Say No to Bullies.* He shoved it into his backpack.

"Oh, Eddy, I'm so sorry, we seem to have run overtime again. I know how much you hate being late for lunch."

"That is fine," said Eddy. He saw Tiffany's eyebrows rise very high and explained. "I got sick of never finishing my lunch, so I changed my lunch routine."

Tiffany gasped as if she were frightened, except she had a big smile on her face. "Eddy, you are just full of surprises today. I know how much you hate change."

"I hate hunger more, so now I just pack a Qwik-E-Meal bar." He pulled one out of the front pocket of his backpack. Chocolate (*Theobroma cacao*) Crunch. "Sometimes change is a good thing."

10. Figures

The weekend flew by as Eddy constructed version 2 of his invention with an elegantly simple detection system. He sealed two pressure switches from washing machines into lengths of garden hose, which he would lay across the road. When a car rolled over the hose, the pressure inside it would increase, sending a signal to the device, which would then make the necessary calculations.

Version 2.1 had only one garden hose detector. Eddy had figured he could determine the time interval between when the front and back wheels hit the detector. He discarded the idea when he realized that the distance between the front and back wheels (the wheelbase) was variable. Not that it varied in an individual vehicle. (Eddy imagined a car with a variable length. It might look like an accordion. That would give a completely new meaning to the term *stretch limo.*) No, what he had realized is that all wheelbases are not the same; they can range from less than 2.5 meters for a subcompact to more than 2.8 meters for a full-sized car, even more for a truck. Without knowing the wheelbase for each vehicle that passed over the detector, he couldn't determine the velocity.

So here was version 2.2, which had two hose detectors. The front wheels of each car would pass over each of the two sensors. He could then measure velocity by dividing the time it took to pass between the sensors by the distance between the sensors. That distance would be constant.

All that remained was to determine the threshold velocity and to build the alarm system itself. At first he thought that a siren of some sort would work, but he decided on something quieter. He added a set of red light-emitting diodes that he could signal to flash. The flashing lights could remind the driver to stop, and alert any pedestrians in the area to impending danger. As an added touch, he rigged up a speaker to play a synthesized voice using parts from the talking toy computer in his junk pile. He had considered making it say something like "Hey! You might hit some little kid, you dodo head!" but he decided a shorter message was better. He settled on "Stop!" but the best he could do was "Thtop!"

Eddy was pleased with his new design, even though this version of the device was much bulkier than the previous version. Two three-meter lengths of garden hose wouldn't fit into his backpack, so he coiled up the hoses and carried them over his shoulders.

He was also pleased that Kip had suggested he use this invention for next year's science fair. He would have almost a year to perfect it. Plus, he could collect enough real-life data to show how effective it is. He could save lives *and* win next year's fair. He would be killing two birds with one stone, which was a disgusting figure of speech.

He spent Sunday calibrating the instrument. He had

intended to figure out the optimum positions for the hoses on paper, but his dad convinced him to determine this experimentally. He needed to see which cars stopped and which cars didn't, and determine the best place to measure velocity. Since the traffic was lighter on Sunday than on weekdays, it took him all day. He filled the time between cars by practicing his Morse code:

Hydrogen, H: ● ● ● ●
Helium, He: ● ● ● ● ●
Lithium, Li: ● — ● ● ● ●
Beryllium, Be: — ● ● ● ●
Boron, B: — ● ● ●
Carbon, C: — ● — ●
Nitrogen, N: — ●
Oxygen, O: — — —
Fluorine, F: ● ● — ●
Neon, Ne: — ● ●

Once he had found the right position for the hoses, he watched the cars to determine the velocity above which the cars were unlikely to stop. At first, he had a lot of difficulty because, as with version 1.0, nearly every car stopped at the stop sign. Suddenly it dawned on him that his presence with the device was the problem. Inventions don't exist in a vacuum; there is always a human element, psychological factors that Eddy often overlooked. When drivers saw Eddy and his device, they slowed down, just as they slow down when they see those signs that use radar to display vehicle speed. Eddy once again wished he could get his hands on a radar gun.

After he moved out of sight behind a white oak tree (*Quercus alba*), the percentage of lawbreakers returned to the numbers he had observed earlier. By the end of the day, he had adjusted the settings so that he could predict with 95 percent accuracy if a car would come to a complete stop.

Fact Number 144 from the Random Access Memory of Edison Thomas: The white oak is the official state tree of Illinois, Connecticut, and Maryland.

Eddy didn't have time to set up the whole device before school the next day, so he just brought the control box to install in the morning. He squatted on the sidewalk next to the stop sign and opened up the access panel. Then he used a U-bolt to attach the box to the stop-sign pole so that nobody would walk off with it.

A pair of hands on his shoulders made him drop the nut he was trying to attach to the end of the U-bolt. The nut fell to the bottom of the control box and rolled under a relay.

"Hey, E.T., how are those quarter-inch nuts of yours?" Eddy could feel Mitch's breath on the back of his ear.

"I am using seven-sixteenth-inch nuts for this application."

"Smaller nuts?"

"Actually, seven-sixteenth-inch nuts are larger than quarter-inch nuts."

Mitch squeezed Eddy's shoulders hard, pushing down on them as he stood up, nearly tipping Eddy over in the process. "Well, then, congratulations! Hey, did you hear that, Will? Eddy has bigger nuts today."

"Bigger nuts," repeated Will, who was standing near Eddy's backpack a few meters away. "Good one, Mitch."

"Well, have fun with your nuts, Professor," said Mitch as he and Will laughed loudly.

Eddy turned and watched Mitch and Will walk toward the school building, thinking about what Justin thought of Mitch. Mitch's words seemed friendly enough. Maybe it was the way he said things' or that sour-apple look on his face that had clued Justin in. He thought about the pamphlet Tiffany had given him. Was Mitch-Man a bully?

Eddy tried to fish the nut from inside the control box, but he couldn't reach it with his fingers. He removed the nut from the other end of the bolt to detach it, turned the control box over, and shook it until the nut fell out. Then he had to reattach both ends of the U-bolt to the box. He finger-tightened the nuts onto the U-bolt, then replaced the access panel. The bell rang. Eddy slipped his nut driver into his back pocket, grabbed his backpack, and headed to school.

Fact Number 2 from the Random Access Memory of Edison Thomas: The coco de mer (*Lodoicea maldivica*), a palm tree native to the Seychelles Islands, produces the world's largest nut. The nut floats only after it has germinated.

The morning was uneventful, and Eddy was confident the new version of his device would work. After school, he would go home to get the detector hoses and install them.

Eddy smelled trouble the minute he walked into the hall outside the lunchroom. They were serving fish sticks for hot lunch. On fish days, the smell in the lunchroom was so strong he couldn't bear to eat there. He turned around and retreated to his favorite quiet, fish-free stairwell.

It was probably just as well that he didn't eat his lunch in the lunchroom that day. He had been trying to convince Justin to learn Morse code, and Justin was resistant to the idea. The last time Eddy brought the subject up, Justin had yelled at him. ("Enough already!")

Eddy still wanted to come up with a way to use Morse code. It wasn't worth learning a code if he couldn't use it with anybody. Maybe he could write his entire biography project in Morse code. But what if Ms. Terwilliger, his English teacher, couldn't understand Morse code? She would probably give him an F (● ● — ●).

"Hey, Eddy. How are you?"

A person with hair the color of malachite (copper carbonate hydroxide) had snuck up beside him.

"Sorry I startled you. Don't you remember me?"

Eddy blinked.

"I'm Terry. You know, Justin's friend. The *Tron* fan."

"Oh. Hi." The green hair had fooled Eddy. He had thought Terry's hair was blue. He also had thought Terry was a boy. Her hair was very short for a girl and she was wearing jeans and a baggy sweatshirt. Eddy took a deep breath and looked at her face. Since looking at people's eyes increased his adrenaline and activated his fight-or-flight response, he looked mostly at Terry's mouth and nose. Eddy decided that, yes, Terry was indeed a girl.

"What are you doing here?" asked Terry.

"Nothing."

"Why aren't you eating lunch?" asked Terry.

"I am. I mean I will. I can not stand the smell of fish in the cafeteria."

"It is pretty gross."

"Fish smells really bother me, even if somebody is eating a tuna fish sandwich near me. Justin sometimes has tuna fish for lunch."

"Did you tell him?"

"Tell him what?"

"That his sandwiches bother you."

"No, I just try to think about something else, or move away." Eddy had thought about some solutions to the problem. A nose plug might work, but it would look conspicuous and people might tease him about it.

"If you told Justin that tuna bothers you," continued Terry, "I'm sure he could bring something else."

The idea hadn't occurred to Eddy. "He sometimes has bologna. That does not bother me at all."

"Well, there you go," said Terry. "And here I go. I have to get this video to Ms. Copeland."

"What is it?"

Terry looked at the cover. "It's called *Sea Squirts and Lancelets, Our Chordate Cousins*. Fascinating stuff."

Eddy was surprised that Terry thought sea squirts were interesting. He wanted to ask her a question about sea squirts, but when he looked up, she had headed up the stairs and turned the corner.

Eddy sat down on the bottom step of the stairwell for his gourmet meal. He unzipped the front pocket of his backpack to get his Qwik-E-Meal bar. He reached in and was surprised that his fingers wrapped around an object too large to be a Qwik-E-Meal bar. He pulled it out and looked at it. His arm felt as if it had been instantly plunged into liquid nitrogen and frozen solid. The cold crept up his arm and spread through his body. If he moved, he would shatter.

It wasn't a Qwik-E-Meal bar at all. It wasn't even food.

It was a flying Tiger Roman Candle.

After what seemed like minutes, he thawed enough to be able to shove the Roman candle quickly back into his backpack. He shivered a little.

Eddy zipped his backpack and looked around to make sure nobody had seen him.

… bromine, krypton, rubidium, strontium …

Fireworks were strictly forbidden at school. Mr. Benton had a zero-tolerance policy. If anyone caught him with the

Roman candle, he would be suspended, automatically. No exceptions.

… *yttrium, zirconium, niobium, molybdenum* …

He would have to get rid of it, put it somewhere that couldn't be traced to him. But where? The garbage. He needed lots of garbage. The lunchroom.

… *technetium, ruthenium* …

Eddy went back toward the lunchroom, hesitated at the door for a second, and held his breath as he entered. He couldn't just throw it in the garbage. He had to hide it somehow.

He found Justin sitting by himself in the usual place, packing up his trash into his lunch bag, apparently getting ready to leave.

"Justin—"

"Hey, where were you?"

"My session with Tiffany ran over again," lied Eddy. He didn't even have a session with Tiffany today. "Are you done with your lunch?"

"Yeah. I'm helping Ms. Copeland set up for science class again. Sorry I can't stay here with you while you eat."

"Here, let me throw your bag away for you."

"Thanks, but I can—"

Eddy grabbed Justin's lunch bag and walked immediately to the boys' room. He went into a stall, locked the door behind him, and sat on the toilet.

… *holmium, erbium, thulium, ytterbium* …

The bathroom door opened and Eddy froze, trying not

to make a sound. Footsteps echoed as someone walked over to use the urinal. Whoever it was did not stop to wash his hands.

... *lutetium, hafnium, tantalum* ...

Once Eddy was sure nobody was in the room, he unzipped his backpack and took out the Roman candle. He examined it closely, wondering how it had gotten there. The wrapper didn't reveal any clues. Just the expected safety warnings and "Made in China."

When he opened up Justin's discarded lunch bag, a wave of nausea hit him so strongly that the back of his tongue stiffened in a barely suppressed gag reflex. Justin hadn't finished his *Thunnus alalunga* sandwich, and the tuna and bread scraps remained unwrapped in the bag. Eddy willed his stomach back down his throat as he placed the firework in the bag, wrapping the empty sandwich bag and greasy napkin around it for good measure.

... *tungsten, rhenium, osmium* ...

The bathroom door opened again. This time noise filtered in from the hall outside. Lunch period was almost over. Two sets of footsteps entered the room. Again, the door opened. More footsteps. Some conversation about the upcoming football game at Drayton High. Eddy was motionless.

It got quieter, but Eddy wasn't absolutely sure he was alone. He zipped his backpack as quietly as he could. He flushed the toilet before he left the stall, so as not to raise suspicion, in case somebody was there. Then he scrubbed his hands very thoroughly to remove both the tuna smell and any traces of black powder that might betray him.

... *actinium, thorium, protactinium* ...

He dried his hands and threw the paper towel away. For a second, he hoped he could end it here, but the bathroom garbage can was nearly empty. Apparently, Eddy was the only person in school who washed his hands after using the bathroom. It had to be the lunchroom, where the half-empty milk cartons, wrappers, and uneaten fruits and vegetables would swallow up the evidence.

It would look very strange if he just walked in and threw the bag away, so he worked his way against the stream of students leaving the lunchroom and easily found a seat at an empty table. He took his Qwik-E-Meal bar (Rocky Road flavor) out of his backpack, unwrapped it, and took a bite, staring at the wrapper while he chewed. And chewed. And chewed. Swallowing was problematic. His esophagus seemed unwilling to accept any food right now.

After one bite of his meal bar, he got up and threw his trash away—the remains of the meal bar and its wrapper into the garbage can that was nearly full, and the bag of contraband explosives and tuna scraps into the half-full can next to it. As more garbage was placed in the can, the Roman candle would be buried in half-eaten fish sticks, tartar sauce, overcooked green beans, and sour milk-soaked napkins. Eddy hoped the large quantity of discarded milk in the can would keep the Roman candle from igniting.

Eddy squeezed through a bunch of giggling girls to get back into the hall.

He exhaled.

He looked around to make sure nobody was watching him, then headed straight for Coach Vang's office.

"May I please use the trampoline?"

"Sure," said Coach Vang, getting his keys out of his pocket. "What's up?"

Eddy looked at the ceiling. "Nothing"

"Are you OK?" Coach Vang unlocked the storage room door.

"Fine." Eddy dropped his backpack next to a pile of tennis rackets and passed Coach Vang without another word. He walked directly to the trampoline and started jumping. It took longer than usual for the rhythm to settle in. Jump. Jump. Jump. What if someone saw him get rid of the Roman candle? How could he explain that he had no idea how it got there? Who would believe him? Jump. Jump. Jump. Coach Vang peeked into the storage room, but Eddy looked away. Jump. Nobody would know about the firework. He had disposed of the evidence before anyone could have known about it. Jump. Jump. He had to focus his mind on something else. Jump. His traffic device.

The bell rang.

Eddy kept jumping. The control unit was all set. He just needed to run home after school to get the hoses and lay them across the road. Jump. Once he hooked them up to the control unit, it would be ready to go. Jump.

"Eddy."

Maybe it would need a little more calibration.

"Eddy, you need to get to class." Coach Vang stood at the storage room door.

"I know," replied Eddy, and he headed off to English class, trying with every neuron in his brain to replace thoughts of the Roman candle with more productive (and less stressful) plans for his traffic device.

Fact Number 568 from the Random Access Memory of Edison Thomas: Gunpowder, or black powder, is composed of carbon (originally obtained from charcoal), sulfur, and potassium nitrate (saltpeter). In its simplest form, the combustion of gunpowder is expressed in the following reaction: $3C + S + 2KNO_3 \rightarrow K_2S + 3CO_2 + N_2$.

CONFLICT

Ms. Terwilliger underlined the word on the blackboard, causing a painful squeak with the chalk. She set the chalk down and wiped the dust off her hands.

"We know that conflict is an essential part of the plot in fiction, but conflict is just as important to compelling nonfiction. Let's look at the different kinds of conflict we might use in our biographies."

Eddy opened his Thomas Edison book to the appendix, where a series of schematic diagrams showed how the original phonograph Edison invented in 1877 had evolved. The first model used a cylinder covered with foil to record and play back the sounds. Later models used wax cylinders. Edison even invented a talking doll that used a very tiny wax cylinder. Maybe Ms. Terwilliger would let him construct a working model of the Edison phonograph instead of writing something. He knew it was possible to make a working model of the Edison phonograph since They Might Be Giants had recorded four songs that way at the Edison Museum.

Ms. Terwilliger's hand tapped the schematic drawing of the original phonograph.

"It's time to work on the lesson," she whispered. "I want you to list the different conflicts in your subject's life. Who is the subject of your biography?"

"Thomas Edison."

"Fine. You can use the list on the board to help you."

Eddy looked at the board.

Character vs. ...

Self

Nature

Society

Another character

That was no help. Eddy flipped through the book. He checked the index under *conflict* and found nothing. He tried the table of contents.

Chapter 8: "The Current War." War sounded like a conflict. Eddy turned to chapter 8 and read about the disagreement between Thomas Edison and Nikola Tesla over the use of alternating current or direct current for the distribution of electrical power. Edison favored DC. Tesla favored AC.

Edison and Tesla repeatedly attempted to discredit each other. Both Edison and Tesla were rumored to have been nominated for the 1915 Nobel Prize in Physics, but neither was willing to accept the prize if he had to share it with the other. In the end, the 1915 prize was awarded to William H. Bragg and his son, William L. Bragg, for their work using X-rays to reveal the structure of crystals.

Neither Edison nor Tesla was ever awarded the Nobel Prize, even though both contributed immensely to our scientific knowledge. Edison's contributions were practical and he became a wealthy man. Tesla's contributions were more theoretical and Tesla died penniless.

Eddy wondered what would have happened if Edison and Tesla had gotten along, or even gotten together. With Tesla's theoretical abilities and Edison's flair for popular inventions, they would have been a great team. Eddy knew a lot about Nikola Tesla, since so much had been named after him. The Tesla is a unit of measurement of magnetic fields (actually of magnetic flux density). Then there is the Tesla coil, which made most modern electronic devices possible.

Even though an eddy coil wasn't anything like a Tesla coil, and even though the eddy coil wasn't actually named after him, Eddy pictured his project that had failed to win the science fair. Eddy had used it to make a copper ring fly through the air. Impressive, but not practical. More like a Tesla invention than an Edison invention. Tesla's ideas were brilliant, but Edison's more useful inventions had earned him all that recognition (and money). Next year, Eddy's very useful traffic device would win first place for sure.

Fact Number 1,500,000 from the Random Access Memory of Edison Thomas: The world's largest conical Tesla coil is in the Mid-America Science Museum in Hot Springs, Arkansas.

When Eddy got to his locker at the end of the day, Mr. Benton stood there waiting for him.

"I have reason to believe that you may be in possession of some illegal materials," said Mr. Benton stiffly.

Hydrogen, helium, lithium …

"What sort of materials?" asked Eddy. He gripped the shoulder straps of his backpack, picturing his adrenal glands pumping out adrenaline, and trying to stop them.

"May I have a look in your locker, please?"

… oxygen, fluorine, neon …

Eddy looked at his locker. He had never cleaned up the ketchup drip on the door. Maybe that was why Mr. Benton knew about the condiment packages. Eddy had removed most of them from his locker, but there might be a few left. Justin was probably right. Mitch had put them there.

Eddy dialed the combination and opened the door.

… sulfur, chlorine, argon …

Eddy pushed at the panic in his head as Mr. Benton pulled the books off the shelf at the top of his locker and peeked behind them.

… cobalt, nickel, copper, zinc…

Mr. Benton rifled through the papers at the bottom of the locker. "Ah," exclaimed Mr. Benton. He had found something.

Panic. Push it back. *Gallium.*

It was just condiments. *Germanium.*

Not a serious offense. *Arsenic.*

Mr. Benton pulled back his hand, which was covered with mustard. He pulled a handkerchief out of his pocket and wiped his hand. "Nothing illegal here," he said. "You really should clean out this locker, young man."

Eddy exhaled. "Yes, sir."

"Now the backpack."

"What?" *Selenium.*

"I need to look in your backpack."

It wasn't the condiments Mr. Benton was looking for. It was the Roman candle. How did he know about it? *Bromine.* Eddy's heart rate spiked, but then he reminded himself that he had already disposed of the evidence. The panic subsided. There was nothing for Mr. Benton to find and nothing for Eddy to fear. He took a cleansing breath, slipped his backpack off his back and onto the floor, unzipped every zipper, and stepped back confidently.

Mr. Benton stared at Eddy's face for a moment, glanced into each compartment of the backpack, then studied Eddy's face again. "False alarm, I suppose. I may have been given some false information. I apologize."

Once Mr. Benton was gone, Eddy rezipped all the

zippers on his backpack. Could this day get any stranger? Who ever heard of a principal apologizing to a student?

Fact Number 5,000,000,000 from the Random Access Memory of Edison Thomas: The term *stool pigeon* is derived from the practice of hunting passenger pigeons (*Ectopistes migratorius*). A stuffed pigeon was placed on a stool as a decoy to attract other pigeons.

By the time Eddy ran home, then carried the detectors for his device back to the intersection, most of the kids had left school.

He set to work, carefully measuring the distance from the stop sign to each of the sites for the detectors. He was glad to have a project that was interesting and complex enough to drive out the Roman candle thoughts.

As he was placing the second detector across the road, Coach Vang came by.

"Hey, Eddy," said Coach Vang. "How's it hanging?"

"Uh, fine," replied Eddy, looking at the hose that was hanging from his hands.

"What are you working on?"

"It is a device to measure the velocity of vehicles as they approach the stop sign. A lot of drivers have been ignoring the sign, you know."

"That's a real problem, I guess."

"Yes, it is. I am thinking I might enter this device in next year's science fair. If I start now, I can collect a large amount of data. That will make the statistics more convincing."

"Great. So how does it work? What are the hoses for?"

"The cars go over them and trip pressure sensors—"

"Oh, like gas stations used to have," interrupted Coach Vang. "When a car rolled over the hose, it rang a bell inside the building so the attendant knew a customer was waiting."

"Exactly like that." Eddy knew he liked Coach Vang for a reason.

"Are you feeling better after your tramp time?" asked Coach Vang.

"Yes, I am fine."

"Is there anything you want to talk about?"

"No." Why would Eddy want to talk about something he was trying to forget?

"Well, then, good luck with your project. I need to go now, but if you decide you want to talk, my door is always open."

"Thank you." Actually, Coach Vang's office door was frequently closed, or even locked.

Eddy let his traffic device absorb his attention again. He finished with the detectors and began installing the control unit next to the pole that held the stop sign, tapping out the elements in Morse code while he worked. The metal pole made a nice ringing sound when he tapped it with his quarter-inch nut driver.

"That's a good beat. Very complex." Kip had a guitar

case in his left hand. "Did you ever think of taking up the drums?"

"No," stated Eddy flatly. "I was doing Morse code."

"Well, maybe you should think about learning drums. You've got a great sense of rhythm."

"I am not very musical."

"Music is just math," said Kip, putting his guitar down.

"As a matter of fact, that is true. Sound waves are vibrations. A musical tone is a collection of related vibration frequencies, and the numerical relationship between the frequencies determines the quality of the tone. Without a whole-number mathematical relationship between the frequencies, it is just noise, not music."

"My mom calls our music noise," said Kip.

Eddy laughed.

"Anyway," continued Kip. "You should come to one of our jam sessions."

Eddy thought of orange (*Citrus sinensis*) marmalade and strawberry (*Fragaria ananassa*) preserves. He was getting hungry.

"Eddy?"

"Yes."

"Would you like to try some jamming with us sometime?" Now Eddy thought of jamming radio signals.

"You know, Eddy, maybe you'd have more friends if you didn't ignore people all the time."

"I do not ignore people."

"Um, yeah, you do. You didn't even say good-bye to me the other day. Were you mad at me for criticizing your invention?"

"No," said Eddy. Why would he be mad at Kip?

Kip looked at his watch. "Yikes! I'm late for practice. It was supposed to start at 7:00."

Eddy looked at his own watch. 7:16:36. He was late for dinner. No wonder he was so hungry. In the light of the streetlamp, he hadn't really noticed how dark it had gotten. He made sure all the components were secure, then packed up and ran home for dinner.

Fact Number 220 from the Random Access Memory of Edison Thomas: The white layer of citrus peels is called the albedo. It is high in pectin, which is used to thicken jams, jellies, and preserves.

11. Stop!

The next day in homeroom, Mr. Benton announced over the intercom system that there would be an assembly at the end of the day, called "Veggies Are Our Friends." Eddy groaned. Not only would the assembly be lame, but the day's schedule would be completely disrupted. Eddy tried frantically to copy the revised schedule from the blackboard (which was actually jade green) onto his own printed schedule. He hated assembly days. He was constantly consulting his revised schedule so he would know what to expect as the day unfolded.

Midmorning, he found himself in an exceptionally crowded and noisy gym. A sharp whistle produced instant silence (and a sharp pain in Eddy's head).

"All right, all right," yelled Coach Vang, bouncing a basketball, the ping of each bounce echoing against the walls of the now quiet gym. "I know it'll be tough with double the students in gym this period, but it's only for one day. Let's settle down and divide up into four groups, one in each corner."

The random and indistinct noise of the crowd started up again as a disorganized migration to each of the corners materialized. Eddy headed to the corner with the fewest

students. He faced the wall for a moment ... *sodium,*
magnesium, aluminum ... Once he had calmed down a little,
he turned around and discovered that Mitch Cooper and Will
Pease had joined his group. A cold, hard knot formed in the
pit of his stomach. How could he face Mitch now?

Coach Vang had instructed the group to form two lines
for passing drills. Eddy hated passing drills, and any other
kind of ball-handling drills, for that matter. When Coach
Vang was hanging around Eddy's corner of the gym, the
drills were merely frustrating. Eddy dropped about half of
the balls passed to him. When Coach Vang was occupied
in another corner, things got worse. Mitch and Will took
turns passing very hard at Eddy's head, knees, and other
sensitive parts, even when it wasn't Eddy's turn to get the
ball. The other kids seemed to think it was funny to watch
Eddy try to avoid being hit. Eddy failed to see the humor
in the situation.

"Hey, Eddy," said Mitch. "This isn't dodge ball. You're
supposed to catch the ball."

"I dunno, Mitch," said Will. "I think Eddy's doing a
bang-up job."

"Yeah," added Mitch. "He's a regular firecracker on the
basketball court."

"Check out his explosive speed," said Will, and he
heaved the ball so hard that Eddy couldn't evade it and he
couldn't catch it. He was barely able to deflect it. The impact
of the ball on his hands left them stinging. He rubbed his
hands together and looked at them. They were red.

Why were Mitch and Will making those fireworks references? Were they responsible for the Roman candle? Eddy had had enough trouble realizing he and Mitch weren't friends anymore. He had finally admitted that Mitch was a jerk, or even a bully. But this was harder to believe. Fireworks were not allowed in school, and Roman candles were illegal. Was Mitch a criminal?

Before Eddy could complete his thought, Coach Vang blew his whistle again. Instinctively, Eddy clapped his hands over his ears, even though the noise had stopped before his hands reached them. "All right, now those of you on this side of the gym, line up at the center line for some lay-up and rebounding drills. The rest of you run laps."

A communal groan filled the gym.

"That's enough," said Coach Vang. "You'll get a chance to shoot some baskets later. Now get going."

Even though Coach Vang had indicated that Eddy, Mitch, and Will were to start with the lay-up drills, Eddy merged into the group running laps. Running laps was definitely better than shooting lay-ups, especially if Mitch and Will were involved. He looked up at Coach Vang to see if he had noticed his evasive maneuver. Coach Vang looked directly at Eddy and nodded.

After gym class, Eddy got to the lunchroom early, claiming his favorite spot in the corner. Coach Vang usually let him cut out a few minutes earlier than the rest of the class, so he was in and out of the locker room before everyone else got there. He was tired, because he had managed to avoid the lay-ups altogether by running laps with both groups. Also, his right sock was wet. When he had changed out of his gym shoes into his regular shoes, there had been a ketchup packet inside, which had burst when he put on the shoe.

Since he had started bringing Qwik-E-Meal bars for lunch, Eddy didn't really need to eat in the lunchroom, but he found himself looking forward to his conversations with Justin. As long as Justin wasn't having tuna fish.

When he opened the front pocket of his backpack to get his Qwik-E-Meal bar, he was relieved that there were no fireworks, but he found the bullying pamphlet that Tiffany had given him. He peeked around the room to make sure nobody was watching him and opened up the pamphlet. It confirmed what Justin had been telling him and what he had begun noticing about Mitch. He usually did his bullying when there weren't any adults around. He always claimed that things happened by accident, like the time he stepped on Eddy's fingers when he was trying to recover Meara's dry-cleaning money, or when he "accidentally" kicked Eddy's nut driver almost into the storm sewer. "Oops!" he'd say. Eddy wondered how many times Mitch had "accidentally" hurt him. Somehow, it was more humiliating now that Eddy knew what had been going on.

But what about the condiments in his locker? How could that be an accident? Or the Roman candle?

Justin approached the table, and Eddy slipped the pamphlet back into his backpack.

"What's that?" asked Justin, unpacking his lunch.

"Nothing," said Eddy. "Just some homework." What would Justin think if he knew that Eddy needed a pamphlet to figure out he'd been the victim of a bully?

"Is math in fifth period or sixth period today?" asked Justin.

Eddy consulted his revised schedule. "Sixth," he said.

"Snap. I hate assembly days," said Justin. "The schedule is always all mixed up. I like math better in the morning."

"I do, too," said Eddy.

Justin reached into his backpack and set his lunch bag on the table, along with a piece of paper. "Look at this," he said. "I found this picture on the Internet last night." He handed Eddy the paper, which was a photograph of a pencil embedded in a tree.

"Oh."

"I'm going to add it to my tornado poster for the regional science fair. I knew tornadoes could do that sort of thing, but I couldn't find a picture of it until now."

Eddy had completely forgotten about this year's science fair. He thought of his eddy coil—the third-place entry that did not earn him the right to be in the regionals. "Are you allowed to make changes like that?"

"It's OK. I asked Mr. Benton about it."

Eddy hesitated. What would it hurt if Justin made his project better? Eddy was out of the competition anyway. If Eddy couldn't compete, at least he could help Justin win. "You could make the tornado easier to see in the chamber with dry ice. That would increase your temperature gradient and it would produce more condensed water vapor."

"That's a great idea," said Justin. "But where can I find dry ice?"

"I usually get mine at the ice cream factory over in Pennington. They will sell you a block. But you have to bring your own cooler."

"Thanks, I'll do that." As Justin unwrapped his sandwich, Eddy smelled tuna.

"Umm, Justin?"

"What?"

"When you have tuna fish for lunch, it makes me nauseous."

"Does it?"

"Yes, I can not eat my own lunch if I smell your tuna."

"Great!" said Justin.

"What?" said Eddy. It was not the response he had expected. Was Justin happy that his sandwiches made Eddy sick?

"Now I have an excuse not to bring tuna," explained Justin. "I would rather have bologna, but my mom says that fish is brain food."

"The omega-3 fatty acids in oily fish are indeed good for your brain and cardiovascular system," said Eddy. "But you should also know that some fish, including canned albacore tuna, or *Thunnus alalunga*, can contain high levels of mercury, which may offset the benefit. Mercury is a heavy metal that can cause brain damage. You can avoid the mercury issue altogether by using an alternative source of omega-3 fatty acids, such as flaxseeds or walnuts."

"Excellent!" said Justin. "It's great to have you as a friend, Eddy. You have an answer for everything."

The fact was that Eddy did not have an answer for everything.

For example, did Mitch really put the Roman candle into his backpack?

If he did it, then how did he do it? And why?

Was there another explanation?

What, if anything, should Eddy do about it?

Should he ask Justin for advice?

No, thought Eddy. The fewer people who knew about it, the less likely he was to get in trouble.

Fact Number 9.80665 from the Random Access Memory of Edison Thomas: The largest freshwater fish ever caught was a Mekong giant catfish (*Pangasianodon gigas*) weighing 646 pounds.

"Veggies Are Our Friends" turned out to be just as lame as Eddy had suspected it would be. People dressed up as vegetables, dancing around and singing about how tasty they were. The assembly was more appropriate for elementary school than middle school. Besides, botanically, tomatoes are fruits, not vegetables, so the whole "Tomato Tornado" production number at the end didn't even belong in the program. This inconsistency, however, was not enough to hold Eddy's interest, and Roman candle thoughts took over (except during the verse of "Tomato Tornado" that referred to ketchup, which also brought back bad memories).

After school, Eddy walked out with Justin. At first, he wanted to ask him what he thought of the Roman candle and how it got into Eddy's backpack, but as much as he now respected Justin's opinion in these matters, it would be wiser to talk about a safe subject. Tiffany said that the weather was always a safe topic for discussion.

"A tornado is a vortex of air that forms in a thunderstorm," said Eddy.

"There are other kinds of weather vortexes," said Justin.

"Vortices," corrected Eddy.

"Anyway, there are gustnadoes and—"

"That is not a real word," said Eddy.

"Yes it is," said Justin. "And you're interrupting me again."

"Sorry," said Eddy.

"Now where was I?"

"Where were you when?"

"Oh, yeah, gustnadoes. There are also cold-weather funnels and waterspouts. Waterspouts are weak tornadoes that form over water. And let's not forget about dust devils."

Eddy forgot about dust devils. "What I do not understand is why a spider" (order Araneida) "would climb up a waterspout. Although it might get sucked up in the inflow winds."

"What do spiders have to do with waterspouts?" asked Justin.

"You know," said Eddy. He extended the index fingers and thumbs of both hands and sang. "'The itsy bitsy spider went up the waterspout ...'" His fingers made the motion of the spider climbing. He stopped when someone bumped into him.

"Is that what they teach you in your 'special classes'? Nursery rhymes?" sneered Mitch. He seemed to be having another laugh with Will and Mark at Eddy's expense.

"Don't pay any attention to him," said Justin. "He's not worth it."

Eddy turned away and tried very hard to disregard Mitch's taunts. Ever since he realized Mitch was a bully, Mitch seemed to be getting meaner. Pushing him harder. Getting him into deeper trouble. Like filling his locker with condiment packages. And planting a Roman candle in his backpack.

Why was Mitch picking on Eddy? The pamphlet said that typical targets of bullying have low self-esteem and poor social skills. Poor social skills. That was Eddy. Why else would he need to have his sessions with Tiffany? Remedial social skills.

"Hey, E.T., here's a new one for you," yelled Mitch. He walked away singing loudly, "The geeky, dorky weirdo went up the waterspout. Down came the—"

"Thtop," droned a synthesized voice from the speaker on the stop sign.

Almost simultaneously, a loud squeal made Eddy clap his hands over his ears. He swung around and saw his invention's lights flashing. At the spot where the sidewalk meets the street, Mitch stood straight and rigid, but teetering a little, as if he were peering over the edge of a cliff. His toes extended two inches into the street from the sidewalk.

In the middle of the crosswalk was a Mastodon 340X sport utility vehicle, stopped right where Mitch would have been, had he kept walking.

Will stood there silently, like a cow (family Bovidae) chewing its cud. Seven girls came rushing toward Mitch, jostling Eddy and Justin out of the way.

Mark began screaming obscenities and ran after the Mastodon as it drove away.

"Mitch!" screamed a tall, skinny girl with hair the color of citrine. "Mitch, are you all right?"

"What happened?" asked another girl.

Eddy flapped his hands ecstatically. "It worked!" he yelled to Justin. "My invention worked!" His chest felt as if it were inflating, like a balloon, crowding out his lungs, so he couldn't breathe.

"Seems that way," said Justin.

Mitch and Mark were still cursing at the Mastodon's driver, even though the car was long gone. A bevy of girls gathered like multicolored butterflies (order Lepidoptera) around Mitch.

"I'm so glad you're all right!"

"You could have been killed!"

"What was that driver thinking?"

Eddy and Justin stood in amazement as Mitch walked away with Will and Mark, followed by the fluttering mob.

"How the snap does he do that?" asked Justin, his mouth gaping open.

"What?" said Eddy.

"Just look at that! He's a girl magnet."

"I would not call him a magnet," replied Eddy. "The attraction is probably hormonal rather than electromagnetic."

Kip ran up to Eddy and Justin. "What's going on?" he asked.

"Eddy's invention worked," said Justin. "Mitch Cooper was almost flattened by a car, but Eddy's contraption saved his life."

"Excellent!" said Kip, holding his hand up in the air. He seemed to be waiting for something, until Justin slapped his hand.

"I'm not sure Eddy's into high-fives," said Justin.

"I like high-fives," said Eddy. "I just did not understand what you were doing."

"Let's try that again," said Kip. "Give me a high-five, Eddy!"

Eddy slapped Kip's newly upraised hand.

"Thtop," lisped the stop sign.

"You've got a problem," said Kip.

"What?" asked Justin. "He's going to become as popular as Mitch? He should be so lucky."

"THTOP," repeated the stop sign.

"No," said Kip. "Your invention is still working."

"That is good," said Eddy, until he looked at it. Not a car in sight.

"THTOP!" Still no cars.

"Oh no," wailed Eddy, slapping his head.

"THTOP!!" Something was definitely wrong.

"There must be some kind of short circuit!" He ran to the corner, dropped his backpack, and rummaged around for his nut driver. He heard Kip and Justin panting as they ran to catch up.

"Having a problem?" asked a deep voice.

"THTOP!!!" said the sign.

Eddy looked down at a pair of shiny black shoes, then he looked up at a Drayton City police officer. According to his badge, his name was Officer Rodriguez.

"No sir," said Eddy, fumbling with the lid to the access panel. "I just need to make a few adjustments to my—"

"THTOP!!!!"

"What is this thing?" asked Officer Rodriguez.

"THTOOOOooooooop!"

Eddy disconnected a couple of wires and stood up, brushing the dirt off his knees. He was happy to explain. Maybe he'd get some kind of commendation or award for service to the city, or a "hometown hero" story in *The Drayton Times*. "It is a device that detects cars going too fast to stop at the stop sign. It works, too. In fact, just now it —"

"It has to come down."

"What?" asked Eddy incredulously. His chest didn't feel so full anymore.

"Your device. It has to come down, son."

"I am not your son," said Eddy.

"Are you kidding?" interjected Kip. "This contraption just saved somebody's life!"

"I saw it, Officer," added Justin.

Officer Rodriguez insisted. "Nevertheless, it needs to come down. You've defaced public property by drilling a hole through the sign."

"I had to," said Eddy. "I needed to mount the light-emitting diodes and speaker."

"In that case, you'll also be receiving a bill for the cost of replacing the sign."

"Give him a break," said Justin.

"Yeah, you tricked him into telling you about the hole in the sign," said Kip.

"I did nothing of the sort. Now you boys get this cleaned up." Officer Rodriguez got out his notepad and a pen. "What's your name, then?"

"Eddy Thomas."

"Is that short for *Edward*?"

"*Edison*," replied Eddy quietly, his good mood now completely deflated.

Justin snorted. "Edison Thomas?"

"You want to make something of it?" asked Kip.

"No," said Justin. "Actually, I like the name Edison. It sounds like somebody that lives in a mansion and rides around in a limo. Edison Thomas the third, millionaire."

"I like the sound of that," said Kip, "especially the millionaire part."

So did Eddy. In fact, being named for someone like Thomas Edison might be a good thing after all, although he would never admit it to Dad.

Officer Rodriguez prompted Eddy to give his address and left. Eddy began removing his invention from the stop sign. "Detention was bad enough," he whined. "But now the police?"

"Look on the bright side," said Kip. "A run-in with the law is considered a rite of passage in some circles."

"Not any circles I would want to be a part of," said Justin, picking up a wrench. "Let's just help him get this thing home."

"Home," groaned Eddy. "My dad is going to ground me for the rest of my life."

"For what?" asked Kip. "Defacing public property? All you'll have to do is pay the fine."

Eddy explained, "When he finds out I drilled through the sign, he will know I borrowed his good cobalt-treated drill bit without his permission. He is always telling me not to use his tools for my inventions."

"That's a problem," said Justin.

Kip rolled up the garden hoses and stacked them on the ground next to Eddy's backpack. "Do you want us to help you carry this stuff home?"

"No, thank you."

Kip and Justin helped Eddy pack up the rest of his things and he trudged home, a coil of hose over each shoulder. The invention seemed a lot heavier now than it did before he installed it. When he got home, Eddy dumped the hoses on the living room floor.

"Get those dirty things out of there," said Mom. "I just shampooed the rug."

Eddy picked up the hoses and threw them down the basement stairs. They clunked noisily on the wooden steps until they hit the concrete floor with a thud.

"What's the matter? Didn't your invention work?"

"Oh, the invention worked fine. I am the failure."

"I'm sure it's not that bad. Here, have a cookie." Mom seemed to think every problem could be solved with a cookie. It wouldn't work this time. This was bigger than a dozen cookies. He needed to do something to improve his mood, but his usual solution of working on an invention was the last thing he wanted to do right now.

"No, thank you," said Eddy. "I am just going to feed O.C."

"O.C.?"

"That is what I call my rabbit now. It is short for *Oryctolagus cuniculus.*

"It's an improvement."

"Is there any lettuce in the fridge?"

"I bought some today. It's on the bottom shelf."

Eddy brought a box of rabbit food and a few leaves of lettuce (*Lactuca sativa*) out to the backyard and opened the rabbit cage. He picked up O.C. and sat on the ground with the rabbit on his lap. He stroked the soft fur behind her ears and tried to organize his thoughts.

All that work. His invention had worked perfectly, at least until it short-circuited (an easily remedied glitch). But what good did it do? What kind of city makes it illegal to protect pedestrians? What a stupid law. Now the cars were going to continue to run the stop sign and endanger innocent lives. Nothing seemed to make any sense. People were even harder to figure out. How was he supposed to know who was being nice to him and who was being mean? They should have signs on their foreheads:

I'm Being Mean, Now.

I'm Not Telling You the Truth.

This Is Sarcasm.

You Can Trust Me.

As if to comfort Eddy, the rabbit looked up at him, then sniffed at his sleeve.

"People should be more like rabbits," Eddy said, stroking her back. "You are a cinch to figure out."

Eddy heard Dad's truck pull into the driveway. It was almost time for dinner. He put O.C. back into the cage and filled the bowl with rabbit food. He put the lettuce into the cage and watched O.C. sniff the leaves and begin to chew on them. Eddy liked to watch her nose wiggle when she was eating. It looked as if she was sucking the lettuce into her mouth. Eddy checked the water bottle and decided it needed a good cleaning. He unhooked it from the side of the cage and emptied it into the grass. He turned to bring it into the house to wash it.

Suddenly, he heard a loud splashing sound and even louder swearing.

"EDISON ALOYSIUS THOMAS!"

Dad must be pretty mad to use Eddy's middle name. Now Eddy saw why. Dad turned the corner into the backyard, soaking wet. He was holding the severed end of a garden hose in his hand.

"How many times have I told you not to use my stuff for your inventions?!"

Eddy decided that answering that question ("Fifty-two") was a bad idea, considering the current volume of Dad's voice.

Fact Number 600,000,000 from the Random Access Memory of Edison Thomas: In 1859, Thomas Austin released a dozen European rabbits (*Oryctolagus cuniculus*) in Australia. By 1910, they had spread over nearly the entire Australian continent. They are responsible for devastating erosion and the extinction of several native plant and animal species. A virus introduced in the 1950s reduced their population, but they remain a serious problem.

12. George Washingtons Cross the Delaware

Eddy lay in the warm water of the bathtub and worked up some lavender-scented lather in his hands. He clenched his fists, then opened them slowly and blew gently, forming a huge bubble between his fingers. He wanted to see the dark area that was supposed to form at the top of a bubble just before it pops. He couldn't see it. His bubble popped, just like his hopes for his invention. He watched the tiny droplets, remnants of the bubble, spread explosively in the air.

There had to be *something* good about the day. Eddy had come up with a solution to the traffic problem, instead of just losing sleep over it. At least Tiffany would be proud. After all, his invention was technically a success, even if Officer Rodriguez didn't think so. Justin and Kip liked it.

Maybe his invention would solve another problem. Since Eddy had saved Mitch's life, Mitch-Man would be eternally grateful to his good buddy Super-Eddy. He might even be proud to be his friend again. Or not. Maybe he would at least stop making fun of Eddy and getting him in trouble. Eddy would settle for that.

Maybe his invention would even make him popular, like Mitch. Eddy hoped not, because he wouldn't like to have so many people around him all the time. He preferred to be by himself, or maybe with one or two other people, like Justin and Kip, or Terry. Otherwise, with too many people talking, Eddy had too many of those stupid, unwritten social rules to decipher at the same time. He held his breath, closed his eyes, and submerged himself in the bathwater. Anyway, he thought, he'd have plenty of time to think about that during his week of extra chores for wrecking Dad's garden hose. Once the bill for the stop sign arrived, it would probably be more like a month.

Fact Number 299,792,458 from the Random Access Memory of Edison Thomas: Reflective signs and paint contain tiny glass beads. Light that hits the surface is reflected directly back where it came from, a process called retroreflection.

The next morning at school, the halls seemed to be noisier than usual, or was it just Eddy's head that was noisy?

"Eddy!"

It was Justin. "Was your dad mad when he found out about the stop sign?"

"I have not told him about it yet." Eddy hoped it would take a week or so for the bill to arrive at his house, since he was already in trouble because of the hose. He hadn't worked up the courage to tell Dad about the Mitch incident.

"Everybody's talking about how your invention saved Mitch's life. That was so great. I mean, snap, even if you had to take it down, you proved that you could do it."

The noise level in the hall increased as a crowd approached. In the center, Eddy could make out Mitch's head protruding about eight centimeters above the others.

This was Eddy's chance. Now Mitch would acknowledge him in front of all these people. His old friend Eddy's ingenious invention had saved his life. "Hey, Mitch!"

The crowd fell silent.

"Hey, geek!" replied Mitch.

The crowd burst into laughter and fluttered away.

Eddy's heart sank. Nothing had changed.

"What's the matter?" asked Justin.

"I thought Mitch would be nicer to me after what happened." Eddy opened his locker.

"You know what they say. A leopard can't change its spots."

Eddy wondered what leopards (*Panthera pardus*) had to do with anything.

"You didn't really expect him to turn into a decent human being, did you?" asked Justin. "Once a jerk, always a jerk. Don't let it bother you."

Mitch hadn't always been a jerk. But he was now.

Eddy looked at Justin. Not everybody was a jerk. Justin wasn't. Justin wouldn't tell on Eddy. "Do you think Mitch is enough of a jerk to plant a Roman candle in my backpack?"

"Snap! Did he do that? When was this?"

Eddy looked around to make sure they wouldn't be overheard. He told Justin the facts about the Roman candle and his suspicions about Mitch.

By the time Eddy had finished talking, Justin's face had turned red. "That explains why you were acting so weird at lunch. You should tell Mr. Benton about it right now!"

"But I do not have any proof that Mitch did anything, and if I tell anybody about it, I could get blamed. And suspended."

"I think you're making a big mistake. If you let him get away with it, what do you think he'll do next?"

"I have no idea what Mitch will do next."

"That was a rhetorical question. I didn't expect you to know the answer."

"Oh."

"I still think you should tell. Mitch needs to know that he can't walk all over you any more."

Eddy pictured himself lying on the ground and Mitch walking on him. That was how he felt lately. Like he had been walked on. "I will think about it."

"Good."

"But promise you will not tell anybody."

"Of course. I'll see you in math class."

Eddy shut his locker door. "Later," he said. He looked at the drip of dried ketchup below the lower ventilation slots of his locker. It looked like blood. He didn't want to give up hope that his traffic invention had mattered to Mitch.

A thought came to Eddy's mind. Every time Mitch said or did anything mean to Eddy, he was with someone else. Not surprising. Mitch was a popular kid and he had a lot of friends. Maybe he really did change his mind about Eddy, but since he was surrounded by admirers, maybe he didn't want to let on that he had a new admiration for Eddy. After all, according to the pamphlet Tiffany had given him, many bullies want other kids to admire them. Or respect them. Or fear them. The other kids were probably encouraging Mitch to do those things. Like Will. He was always hanging around Mitch and laughing at his jokes. Maybe Will was egging Mitch on, although actual eggs were probably not involved.

Instead of going right to homeroom, Eddy headed up the stairs for a detour—a detour past Mitch's locker.

Mitch was alone at his locker. Eddy didn't approach him right away but watched him as he rifled through some papers in his locker, evidently looking for something.

Eddy knew he had to act now, or he'd lose his nerve. He took a deep breath, pasted a smile onto his face, and walked up to Mitch.

"Hey, Mitch-Man."

"What do you want, Super-Dork?"

Mitch had remembered their superhero names. Sort of. That was a good sign. "It was lucky that my invention was there when that SUV blew through the stop sign."

"What?"

"You know," said Eddy. "My traffic control device. It kept you from getting hurt at the intersection."

"So?"

"I just thought you might … have something to say to me."

"Yeah, get lost."

Eddy stood there awhile and mustered up some more courage. "I think this changes things. Do you agree?"

"What would change? You're still a loser. Now get out of my face before I really get mad."

That was it. The last shred of hope Eddy had for the friendship was gone. There was nothing left for him to hold on to. Once he realized that, Eddy expected to feel as if he had lost a friend. Like when his first pet, a gerbil (*Meriones unguiculatus*), had died.

But he didn't. Instead, he felt … relief. As if a heavy burden had been lifted. Eddy didn't have to carry the weight of his friendship with Mitch. He was suddenly, and unexpectedly, free from the notion that he had to put up with Mitch's abuse. He didn't have to do anything to make Mitch his friend. It just didn't matter. In fact, Mitch wasn't even the kind of person Eddy wanted as a friend. He would not be able to change Mitch's attitude, but he could change his own.

The last page of the pamphlet appeared in his mind. He began to recite the speech he had prepared. "I may not be as popular as you—"

"Tell me something I don't know," said Mitch as he found what he had been looking for in his locker and closed the door.

"The square root of 1,225 is 35, but do not change the subject. I may not be as popular as you are, but I am a human being—"

"That's debatable."

"I am a human being and I deserve respect. I want you to stop bothering me and stop making fun of me and getting me in trouble."

"Getting you in trouble?"

"Yes, filling up my locker with ketchup packs."

"What makes you think it was me, Captain Ketchup?"

"And you also put … something … in my backpack."

"Did I?"

"Yes, I believe you did."

"You were always a smart guy, Professor," Mitch laughed as he walked past Eddy, pushing him hard against the lockers. Eddy tried not to yell as he crashed into the lockers, making a painfully loud noise. As he watched Mitch walk away, Eddy realized that he was experiencing a full-blown fight-or-flight response.

… *zinc, gallium, germanium, arsenic* …

Was Mitch admitting to planting the Roman candle?

He closed his eyes and took three slow, deep breaths.

What had he done? He had stood up for himself. He had accused Mitch of a crime. Had he made things worse? He was developing a painful egg-sized bruise on his elbow. Yes, things were definitely worse.

Fact Number 24 from the Random Access Memory of Edison Thomas: The egg of the ostrich (*Struthio camelus*) contains the largest single cell on Earth.

Eddy got to lunch in time to get a table to himself in the

corner. Unfortunately, Justin found him. "Have you gotten over your funk?" he asked.

"No, I am still funky," replied Eddy. He didn't want to tell Justin what had happened with Mitch.

"Funky." Justin laughed. "Snap, Eddy, you crack me up."

Eddy turned to face Justin. He looked him straight in the nose and asked, "Why do you have to laugh at me?"

"Because you're funny!"

"Does that mean you have to make fun of me?"

"I'm not laughing AT you, I'm laughing WITH you."

"I am not laughing, so how can you be laughing with me?"

"No offense, Eddy, but you say some pretty funny things. I'm just laughing at your jokes."

"But I was not telling a joke."

"Maybe you should. You can say some pretty funny stuff. People like that."

Eddy stopped himself from saying anything more. Eddy didn't remember ever having told Justin a joke. Eddy liked to tell jokes, but nobody ever understood them. At least his parents never did.

"See if you like this joke. A ship is sailing around the coast of Madagascar. It is night, but the moon is full. The captain notices an animal in the woods on the island. It has big eyes that glow in the moonlight. The captain calls to his science officer, 'What is that animal?' and the science officer replies, 'Aye-aye, Captain.'"

Justin laughed so hard, his milk spurted out of his nose.

"'Aye-aye.' Like the lemur, right? That's what I'm talking about," he said. "That's hilarious." He wiped his face with his shirt.

Terry approached the table and sat down across from Eddy and Justin. Today her hair was the color of amethyst, a variety of quartz, or silicon dioxide. "Eddy, I hear you saved Mitch's life," she said. "You're a hero!"

"Mitch does not seem to think so," said Eddy, rubbing his sore elbow.

"Well, I do," said Terry. "Guess what?"

"Let me see," mused Justin. "Purple is not your natural hair color. Did I guess right?"

Terry punched Justin in the arm. "No, all the kids are talking about the way Mitch almost got hit by a car, and they say the intersection is too dangerous without a crossing guard."

"Well, duh," said Justin.

"So they decided to do something about it," continued Terry. "They're going to start a volunteer crossing guard squad."

"Oh, right," said Justin. "The crossing guard's been gone for weeks, and nobody notices until the most popular kid in school almost buys the farm?"

"What farm?" asked Eddy.

"Almost croaks," said Justin.

Eddy thought about frogs (family Ranidae) and toads (family Bufonidae). Some croak, but others make more of a chirping sound. In some species, only the male croaks. They croak to claim territory or to attract a mate.

"So who's on this squad?" asked Justin.

"Just the most popular kids, Su Lin and Meara and Maria and Tyrone and Keir ..."

"Who's Kira?" asked Justin.

"Not Kira. Keir," said Terry. "K-E-I-R."

"As in Keir Dullea?" asked Eddy.

"Yeah," said Terry. "'Open the pod bay doors, HAL.'"

"You lost me," said Justin.

"*2001: A Space Odyssey*," said Terry.

"1968. Directed by Stanley Kubrick," added Eddy.

"You guys are weird," said Justin.

Eddy stopped to think. Was that an insult?

"That's why you hang out with us, isn't it?" said Terry.

"Yeah," said Justin.

Probably not an insult, concluded Eddy. He bit into his Qwik-E-Meal bar.

"What are you eating?" asked Terry.

"Oh, it is just my lunch."

"Ah, lembas bread," said Terry.

"It is not bread," said Eddy. "It is a Qwik-E-Meal bar."

"I figured it was something like that. I call those things lembas bread, like in *The Lord of the Rings*. Elves used it for food when they were traveling."

"Oh," said Eddy. The Special Extended Edition DVDs of *The Lord of the Rings* had especially detailed special features. The movie had nothing to do with Eddy's Qwik-E-Meal bar, which was made by the KayZee Natural Foods Company in Kalamazoo, Michigan, not by elves.

Meara McCabe came up to the table. "Terry," said Meara, "can you do crossing guard duty Tuesday afternoons instead of Wednesdays?"

"Oh, so Terry's one of the popular kids now?" asked Justin.

"What can I say?" said Terry as she buffed her fingernails on her sweatshirt and held her hand out as if to admire them. They were the exact purple color of her hair. "You've either got it or you ain't."

"Well?" asked Meara. "Can you?"

"I'm afraid not," said Terry. "I am otherwise engaged."

"Sheesh," muttered Justin under his breath to Eddy. "Get a load of Queen Terry."

Meara sighed. "Well, Bill can't do Tuesdays or Thursdays because he has Tae Kwon Do after school. Jonelle can't do mornings or afternoons every other week because she stays at her dad's house. And Keisha can do mornings, but not afternoons. We'll never get this figured out."

"Sure you will," said Eddy. "You just need to set up a simple spreadsheet."

"Simple?" said Meara.

"All it takes is a couple of macros to sort through your data."

"Umm, Eddy?" said Meara quietly. "Do you think you could do it for us?"

"Sure, when do you need it by?"

"Next week."

"No problem."

Meara dropped a stack of random papers in front of Eddy. "Thanks!" she chirped and walked away.

Eddy straightened out the papers, then hesitated as he thought of something. "Justin?" asked Eddy. "Do you think Meara is trying to get me in trouble by asking me to do this?"

"No, I think you'd really be helping her out."

Eddy smiled to himself. Maybe his invention had worked after all. It hadn't solved the problem in the way he had anticipated, but if it hadn't saved Mitch, the kids at school would never have started up this volunteer crossing guard squad. It was a simple idea. Why hadn't Eddy thought of it? Because it was a simple idea, because it didn't involve a gadget, and because it would have required him to interact with a lot of people. That's why.

"So does this crossing guard squad have a name?" asked Justin.

"The George Washingtons," replied Terry.

"I don't get it," said Justin.

"The intersection is at Delaware Avenue and Hatteras Street."

"So?"

"Didn't you ever hear the story of George Washington crossing the Delaware?"

A sudden, loud laugh escaped from Eddy's mouth. "I get it!" he said.

Fact Number 2,400 from the Random Access Memory of Edison Thomas: *Washington Crossing the Delaware,* painted in

1851 by Emanuel Leutze, contains several errors, including the wrong boat and the wrong flag. In addition, Washington could not possibly have made the crossing standing up.

For the rest of the day, Eddy was grateful to have another detailed task to occupy his mind. The George Washingtons' schedule filled Eddy's head during his free time (and during classes). He immersed himself in the programming, just as he would immerse himself in a swimming pool. When he was submerged in code, the noise from the rest of the world was barely audible. By the time the school day was over, he was ready to write the program, enter the data into his computer, and print out a schedule.

Eddy left school pleasantly motivated to begin the task, but he stopped and felt his stomach twist as he saw the hole he had drilled in the stop sign. He would have to tell Dad before the bill arrived in the mail.

"Eddy, wait up!" It was Kip. "Did you write down the social studies assignment? What are we supposed to read?"

Eddy got his schedule out of his pocket. He had at least paid enough attention in social studies to write the assignment down. "Pages 135 to 152. It is about the Bill of Rights."

"Bill of Rights. Gotcha."

Eddy wondered if Kip liked jokes, too. "Did you know that sleeveless shirts are protected by the Constitution?"

"Sleeveless shirts?"

"Yes, the Second Amendment guarantees the right to

bare arms." Eddy rubbed his right hand up and down his left arm to make sure Kip got the joke.

Kip laughed. "Good one, Eddy."

"Thank you."

"I hear you're helping out with the George Washingtons."

"Yes," said Eddy. "They really are not very organized."

"You'll whip them into shape."

Eddy pushed an unpleasant picture of himself with a bullwhip out of his head.

"Listen, Eddy. My band is playing at a party on Saturday night. Do you want to come?"

Eddy hadn't been to a party in years. Was he popular now? He was about to say yes but decided to ask a question instead.

"Will there be a lot of people there?"

"Sure!" said Kip. "The place will be packed. Everybody loves Western Blot. And what's not to love?"

Packed. Full of people. Way too many social cues to decode. A live band. Probably a very loud band.

"No," said Eddy. He paused, and then added, "I do not like noisy places."

"Are you saying that my band plays nothing but noise?"

"No. Loud sounds bother me."

"I was kidding, Eddy."

"EDDY!" Mr. Benton ran toward them. Eddy's heart began to race. Why was he in trouble this time?

"Eddy, I'm glad ... I caught you." Mr. Benton breathed heavily and bent over, clutching his side.

It was too late to run away. Eddy didn't say anything but waited for the principal to catch his breath. He was glad Kip stayed.

Mr. Benton wiped his brow. "I wanted to catch you before you left for the day. I just got word that Keisha Davis will not be able to attend the regional science competition on Saturday. Her grandmother has passed away."

"Excellent!" said Eddy. An elbow dug into his ribs.

"Say you're sorry to hear about Keisha's grandmother," whispered Kip.

"I am sorry to hear about Keisha's grandmother," repeated Eddy.

"Yes, apparently it was quite sudden," said Mr. Benton. "Because the funeral is Saturday, you'll have to take her place. I wanted to tell you as soon as possible, since you have less than forty-eight hours to prepare. Will you be able to attend?"

"I suppose so," said Eddy.

"Very well. I'll let them know you'll be there. Congratulations, Eddy."

"Thank you," said Eddy.

"I guess that lets you off the hook," said Kip as Mr. Benton walked away.

"What hook?" asked Eddy. Captain Hook. Fishhook. Crochet hook.

"The science fair regionals are definitely a better gig than the party. You don't have to use that lame excuse that we're too loud."

"I did not mean that you were too loud, I just meant—"

"Kidding. See you tomorrow."

Eddy realized that he suddenly had a lot to do. He had promised Meara that he would finish the George Washingtons' spreadsheet by next week. More importantly, he had to find his eddy coil and get it ready for regionals. With so much to do, Eddy wasted no time getting home and getting to work. He did, however, take the time to stop and look both ways before he crossed Delaware Avenue.

13. Change of Plans

Eddy rushed to the basement to find his eddy coil. He knew it must be in the far corner of the basement, in the new pile that he was calling "Underappreciated Inventions." He pulled the coiled-up hoses from his traffic-control device off the top of the pile.

The eddy coil was still in the cardboard box he had used to carry it home from the science fair, untouched for weeks. He pulled the poster and transformer out of the box and examined the eddy coil underneath. The outer layers of wire had been damaged when he had dropped the transformer on top of it. It would take a while to rewind them properly. The transformer was fine. And the poster ...

The poster was ruined. Not only had he crumpled it up when he had stuffed it into the box, but it had gotten wet from the walk home in the rain. The ink had run, the glue had dissolved, and the paper had deteriorated in places. The edges were mildewed.

It was unsalvageable. He couldn't possibly fix the coil and make a new poster in time for the regionals. He would have to tell Mr. Benton that he couldn't attend after all.

Eddy tried to get over his disappointment by telling

himself that the regionals would probably be even noisier than the Drayton Middle School Science Fair. It didn't work. He looked at the pile of disintegrated paper, feeling as crushed as the poster.

Fortunately, he had some programming to do for the George Washingtons. When he was writing computer code, his brain was unable to pay attention to anything else. Eddy immersed himself in programming the volunteer crossing guard schedule. By bedtime, he had printed out the George Washingtons' schedule for the next month, along with his own schedule for the next day.

Fact Number 17,468 from the Random Access Memory of Edison Thomas: The first electronic programmable computer was ENIAC, which stands for Electronic Numerical Integrator and Computer. It made its debut in 1946 at the University of Pennsylvania. It measured 8.5 feet by 3 feet by 80 feet.

"You're crazy," said Justin, closing his locker.

"No, really. It is fine. I did not really want to go, anyway."

"Of course you want to go. It's regionals. There are bound to be some very cool projects there."

Eddy hadn't thought of that. These will be the projects that come in first or second (or third) in their categories. The lame projects will have been weeded out. Like weeds plucked out of a garden. Leaving only the finest specimens.

He might even pick up some hints on making next year's fair project even better and, more importantly, even more appealing to the judges.

"Besides," added Justin, "it'll be you and me representing good old Drayton Middle School. You don't want to leave me to do it all by myself. We have the honor of the school to uphold."

"I did not mean to—"

"You have twenty-four hours to pull something together. I'm sure you can do it."

"The poster is completely destroyed. And it is not just the poster. I need to repair the coil, too. That could take some time."

"Oh, snap, that's a problem. What if … WAIT!"

"What?"

"Come with me." Justin rushed down the hall. Eddy didn't catch up until he got to the principal's office.

Ms. Yamada looked up from her computer. "I'm sorry," she said. "Mr. Benton is in a meeting right now. Would you like to sit and wait?"

"Sure," said Justin, and he led Eddy over to the chairs along the wall.

Eddy didn't like waiting outside the principal's office. It usually meant he was in trouble.

"What is this all about?" he asked Justin as they sat.

Justin leaned over toward Eddy and said quietly, "Your traffic thingy. You can use that instead of the coil."

"But I have no poster for it." His plan had been to use

the device in next year's fair. It would take a lot of work to get it ready by Saturday.

"Oh, yeah. Well, maybe I can help you make one."

"Why would you want to help me? You will be in the competition also."

"So?"

"You want to win."

"Sure," said Justin. "Who doesn't?"

"If you want to win, you would not help me."

"Of course I would. I mean, you're in a pickle."

Eddy pictured cucumbers (*Cucumis sativus*), although many other vegetables, and even fruits, can be pickled.

"Besides," continued Justin, "my tornado chamber is much better now that I'm using the dry ice, like you suggested."

"But if you help me and my project wins—"

"Ooooh, is that a challenge?"

"No, but you will feel bad if I win and you do not win."

"I'd be disappointed, but I'll survive. Let's make a pact. If either of us wins, we celebrate our victory together."

"How?"

"What about a party?"

"I do not know—"

Mr. Benton's door opened, and Will Pease walked out. He glanced at Eddy and Justin and walked quickly out into the hallway without a word. Then Mr. Benton came out of his office, handed Ms. Yamada a sheet of paper, and noticed Eddy and Justin.

"You boys ready for the science fair tomorrow?"

"That's what we came to talk to you about," said Justin. "Eddy has a problem. His project has been damaged. Can he enter another project?"

"It is a device for detecting cars that run stop signs," added Eddy.

"That sounds very interesting, Eddy," said Mr. Benton. "But I'm afraid the rules state that it must be the same project."

"Snap," said Justin.

"Language, Mr. Peterson," warned Mr. Benton. He turned to Eddy. "Is there any way to fix the project in time?"

Eddy thought for a moment. "I can rewind the coil relatively quickly, but I need to start over with the poster."

"Oh, dear. In that case ..."

"Can I help him make a new one?" asked Justin.

Mr. Benton hesitated. "Well, I suppose a little help wouldn't hurt. These are unusual circumstances, after all." The bell rang. "Shouldn't you boys be in class?"

Fact Number 4.6 from the Random Access Memory of Edison Thomas: Food can be pickled either by placing it in vinegar (acetic acid) or by anaerobic fermentation in a salt solution to produce lactic acid. The acidity prevents spoilage.

All morning, Eddy found it harder than usual to concentrate in class. He wished he had his coil with him so that he could rewind it during wasted class time. Instead, he thought about ways to improve the project. Maybe he could add a light bulb mounted on a coil of copper wire. It would light up when it passed near the eddy coil. The coils wouldn't even have to touch. He had all the materials he needed. It wouldn't take too long to put together. By lunchtime, he had constructed the new coil in his head dozens of times.

"Yeah, but what about the poster?" Justin inquired, unwrapping his bologna sandwich. "You need to make a whole new poster and not waste too much time on the coil." Justin sounded disturbingly like Dad when he said that.

"I can just print out the files I used for the Drayton science fair."

"You could, but why not make it better?"

"How?"

Justin thought for a moment. "What about a practical application? Is this coil used for anything besides making stuff fly around?"

"Well, eddy coils are used in recycling plants to separate ferrous from nonferrous metals."

"Great," said Justin. "The judges will love it, especially the green part."

"The coil has no green parts. It is made of iron and copper and some electrical tape, but that is black. Should I try to find green tape?"

"I mean the environmentally friendly part, you know, the recycling."

Meara walked up to the table, which reminded Eddy

that he had brought the George Washingtons' schedule. He pulled it out of his backpack and handed it to Meara.

Meara did not smile as Eddy had expected her to. "Thanks," she said quietly. "The thing is, some of the kids have already asked for changes. I'm sorry."

"That is not a problem," said Eddy. "The program I wrote can easily accommodate changes. What are the changes?" Eddy readied a pencil.

"Oh, I don't have them with me," said Meara. "Can I e-mail them to you?"

"Certainly." Eddy wrote his e-mail address on the paper schedule and handed it back to Meara.

"Great. I'll send it to you when I get home." She bounced away.

"Snap, Eddy. You never told me you had e-mail."

"Of course I have e-mail." But he had never used e-mail to correspond with human beings. He needed an e-mail address to order parts for his inventions and to access content on some of his favorite science Web sites. And he had subscribed to a couple of e-mail newsletters so he could get the latest news on his favorite topics.

"Well, you never e-mail me."

"You never gave me your address." Eddy had never had any reason to e-mail a friend before. Mitch had never given him his e-mail address.

"Well, here it is: j-u-s—"

"Wait." Eddy got his daily schedule out of his pocket and wrote Justin's e-mail. Then he tore off the bottom corner of the paper, wrote his own e-mail address on it, and handed it to Justin.

Fact Number 10^{100} from the Random Access Memory of Edison Thomas: The original name for the search engine Google was *BackRub*.

All afternoon, plans for the poster filled Eddy's mind. He thought of how metals act when the coil is hooked up to an alternating current. Some metals are attracted and some are repelled. He could make rings of different metals to show how the coil would work to separate metals in a recycling plant.

Before he went to his locker at the end of the day, he pulled his schedule out of his back pocket. As he suspected, he had forgotten one last thing. He needed to stop at the art room and pick up his painting. Earlier in the week, he had painted a very elaborate depiction of the rings of Saturn. He had wanted the background—the space beyond the rings—to be very, very dark, like the vast, cold, empty vacuum of space, without a hint of light. He had layered the black paint on so thickly that it had taken a few extra days to dry thoroughly.

He retrieved the painting and turned left out of the art room into the hall, carrying his painting very carefully in both hands.

"Hey, E.T.!" It was Mitch. Eddy ignored him.

"Hey, dork!" Mitch was persistent. Eddy kept walking, increasing his pace. Mitch caught up to him and grabbed him roughly by the shoulder. Eddy turned toward him and just looked at him, but not at his eyes. He was still Mitch, but he looked different, like a stranger. Eddy didn't feel the need to greet him, or even acknowledge him at all.

"Whatcha got there, some finger painting?" said Mitch.

"No," said Eddy.

"Aw, c'mon, let me see it. Did you paint some bunnies or maybe a choo-choo?"

"Actually, it is a—" Eddy stopped himself. He didn't need to explain anything to Mitch. Eddy turned to walk away. His heart rate was beginning to increase. Adrenaline flowed through his veins.

"Lemme see it, Super-Dork," said Mitch, and he grabbed at the painting. Some of the black paint chipped off and fell to the floor.

Eddy managed to wrest the painting back with little additional damage. "Leave me alone," he said firmly. He walked quickly away to his locker, not looking back.

... platinum, gold, mercury ...

When he reached his locker, his heart rate was starting to decrease. The fight-or-flight response had almost subsided. By the time he packed up his backpack, his heart rate was back to normal. Until someone walked up behind him.

"What is that?" asked Justin.

Eddy held up his painting. "It is a depiction of the rings of Saturn set against the blackness of space."

"Are the rings really that brightly colored?"

"Not really," said Eddy. "These colors represent temperature variations in the rings in an image taken by the Cassini spacecraft."

"Very cool," said Justin. "Do you still want me to help you get your project ready for regionals?"

"Yes, that would be nice."

"I need to go home first, but I'll get my bike and come over as soon as I can."

"Do you know where I live?"

"Over on Cherokee, right?"

"Yes. It is a yellow house with a large *Acer saccharinum*, I mean a silver maple tree in the front yard. Look for a squirrel feeder with corncobs hanging from the tree. It is difficult to miss."

"Then I'll see you in about half an hour."

"Thank you." Eddy stood and watched Justin walk away before he headed home himself.

14. Unwind and Rewind

As soon as he got home, Eddy dropped his backpack and retrieved the eddy coil from its box in the basement. He had a lot of work to do. He clamped a metal rod into his bench vise and slid the pipe holding the eddy coil onto it. Then he rigged up an old wire spool onto his cordless drill. He peeled off a little bit of wire from the coil and wrapped it around the spool to get it started. Then he turned on the drill and the spool started spinning, pulling the wire off the coil as the pipe spun around on its rod. Even though he worked slowly and carefully, it took only a few minutes to unwind the first layer of wire. Then he ripped off the electrical tape that separated the layers of wire, exposing the second layer.

The light on his intercom blinked and Eddy stopped what he was doing until Mom's voice came through.

"There's a boy named Justin at the door. He says you're expecting him."

"He is a friend from school. Send him down," replied Eddy.

A few seconds later, Justin came down the stairs and headed straight for the labeled drawers along the wall.

"Snap! This is some setup you've got here. What's all this stuff?"

"Parts that I have salvaged from junk that I found and from old equipment my dad brings home from work." Eddy continued to work on the coil. The second layer of wire was damaged, so he started unwinding it.

Justin turned his attention to the junk pile. He picked up a spectrophotometer. "What the snap is this thing?"

"Please do not touch it."

"Sorry." He put it down carefully. "So what can I do to help? Do you want me to take a turn with the coil?"

"No. It needs to be done very carefully." Eddy continued unwinding the second layer.

"I can be very careful."

"I would rather do it myself."

"Suit yourself. What about the poster? Can I work on that?"

"I suppose so."

"Great. Let's start with your old poster. Where is it?"

Eddy stopped the drill and pointed to the soggy cardboard box in the corner. Justin picked up a corner of the poster. The rest of the poster fell away, back into the box.

Justin dropped the corner of the poster. "You weren't kidding about it being ruined. This is really gross."

Eddy resumed unwinding as Justin reassembled the pieces of the poster on the basement floor, with the occasional "Ick!" as he came across a particularly disgusting wad of disintegrated paper.

By the time Eddy unwound all of the damaged layers of wire from the coil, Justin had re-created a reasonable approximation of the poster. He stood over it, hands on his hips, and sighed, "Not much to work with. I think the diagram is fine. Do you still have that on your computer?"

"Yes. It is on my laptop." Eddy's original poster had a detailed diagram showing how the electromagnetic currents flow around the coil.

"Great, we just need to print a new copy. Otherwise, I think we need to start from scratch. Where can we work on this?"

"I have my laptop set up to access the Internet in the living room. I am not allowed to go online in my room."

"Me neither."

Eddy disconnected his coil-unwinding apparatus and carried his coil with the spool of wire and a roll of electrical tape upstairs. Justin followed. The smells wafting from the kitchen told Eddy that his mom was roasting a chicken (*Gallus domesticus*).

After setting Justin up online, Eddy sat down on the couch to begin the tedious process of rewinding the coil.

"I like your idea of eddy coils in recycling plants," said Justin. "Where should I start the search?"

Eddy didn't look up from his coil. "Try *electromagnetic, recycle, eddy.*"

Justin typed. Eddy wound wire.

"Here's something," said Justin. "But is says *eddy current*, not *eddy coil.*"

"It is the same thing. Is there an image?"

Justin clicked around. "No, just some equations."

From the kitchen, Eddy heard cabinet doors opening

and closing and hard objects clattering on the kitchen counter. What was Mom up to now? The doorbell rang and the clattering stopped.

Mom's voice came into the living room. "Eddy, do you know anyone with purple hair?"

As a matter of fact, he did, although he wasn't expecting her. "It is Terry. Tell her we are in the living room."

Mom showed Terry into the room, saying, "You certainly are popular today, Eddy. I can't remember the last time you had so many friends over."

Eddy thought about that. He had never had so many friends. Period.

"Hey," said Terry. "Justin told me you needed some help with your poster."

"I hope that's OK," said Justin.

"Fine," muttered Eddy, feeling both irritated that Justin had told her he needed help and glad for the help.

Terry looked over Justin's shoulder. "What is all that stuff?"

"I'm looking for a picture of an eddy coil in a recycling plant. Eddy wants to add some practical applications to his poster."

"What does an eddy coil do in a recycling plant?"

Eddy looked up from his coil. "It separates the metals. When you run an electrical current through it, it will attract ferrous metals."

Justin explained. "Ferrous metals are metals that contain iron."

"Technically," corrected Eddy. "Nickel is a ferrous metal, even though it does not contain iron. It is attracted to a magnet."

"What he said," said Justin.

"So an eddy coil is just a magnet?" asked Terry. "Why don't they just use magnets in recycling plants?"

"That is what is so great about eddy coils," said Eddy. "If the metal is nonferrous, like aluminum, and you are using alternating current, the eddy current will repel it. So aluminum cans would be propelled into another container and the steel cans would stay there. The propulsion can be quite forceful. My eddy coil can shoot a copper ring all the way to the ceiling of the gym."

"Oh, I get it!" said Terry. "It's a mass driver!"

"A what?" said Justin.

"A mass driver," repeated Terry. "They use them in science fiction and video games all the time. You use them to launch stuff from other planets."

"The use of electromagnetic coils to launch projectiles in space is purely speculative," said Eddy, "although research is being conducted in the area." Eddy had finished winding a layer of wire, so he started wrapping the coil with electrical tape.

"You should put that on your poster," said Justin. "Let me see what I can find on the Internet." He typed in *mass driver.*

"They're sometimes called electromagnetic catapults," added Terry.

Eddy protested. "This is a real science fair, not a fiction

science fair. I do not think video games count as science." He thought about Mitch's science fair project, which had been a video game. He could not imagine that Mitch would ever come over to his house to help him with a science fair project. He wouldn't be much help anyway, judging by his video game project.

"Don't be such a stick in the mud," said Terry.

"I do not know what mud has to do with anything."

"I mean, use your imagination. You can talk about the POTENTIAL uses of the coil thing. That would get the judges excited."

Justin had been searching for a picture of a mass driver. "I'm not finding anything. Just pictures of car crashes."

"What?" said Terry and Eddy simultaneously. Terry punched Eddy in the arm.

"Please do not hit me," said Eddy.

"Sorry," said Terry. "I just did it because we said the same thing. Great minds think alike."

Eddy didn't agree. After all, look at Edison and Tesla. They both had great minds, but they didn't think alike. That was probably a good thing, because if every great inventor thought alike, then they would all invent the same things.

Terry looked over Justin's shoulder at the laptop screen. "Here's your problem. You spelled *mass* wrong. You were searching for mess drivers."

Justin laughed. "Hey, Eddy, you should invent a mess driver. It could clean up a room by launching dirty clothes off the floor into the laundry."

Terry chuckled. "You could use one of those, Justin. I have never seen a messier room. It's disgusting."

"Such a REPULSIVE task would require a mess driver to produce very strong REPULSIVE forces," said Eddy.

Justin and Terry nearly doubled over with laughter. Eddy felt his skin stretch as a broad smile formed on his face.

"Wait, wait, wait," said Justin, trying to control his laughter. "Aaaaah, watch out for flying underwear! Unidentified flying boxers."

"The problem with flying underwear," said Eddy. "Is just that it would not provide a long-term solution to the problem."

Justin and Terry stopped laughing and looked at Eddy.

"Why?" asked Justin.

"It would only work for a BRIEF time."

Justin groaned. "Oh no, Eddy. That was a really bad pun."

"I thought it was good," Terry laughed. "Sometimes the best puns are the worst ones."

That statement made no sense at all to Eddy.

"All right. Let's get back to work," said Justin. "Why don't we print out what you have already and work from there?"

"That reminds me," said Eddy. "MOM!"

"I'm in the kitchen. Come here and talk to me."

He set the coil on the couch and found his mother standing at the kitchen counter, hands on her hips, surveying a field of little glass jars.

"Umm, Mom? What are you doing?"

"Oh, I'm putting these spices in order. Just look at this. Nutmeg was before cloves. And the tarragon! It's all the way over here, next to the basil. That just doesn't make any sense. But where should I put the coriander? I mean, technically it's the same plant as cilantro."

"*Coriandrum sativum*," said Eddy.

"Exactly. But coriander is the seed."

"Mom."

"And cilantro is the leaf."

"Mom."

"So should I put them together?"

"Mom, can I use your printer for my science fair poster?"

"What science fair? Isn't that over with?"

"No, Mom. It is for the regional competition. I need to regenerate the poster."

"Oh, I guess so. If it's for something important. I don't have any projects going right now."

"Thank you!" said Eddy.

As he left the kitchen, Mom yelled after him, "But don't mess anything up. I just cleaned in there."

Justin and Terry were hunched over the laptop. They looked up when Eddy told them the good news. "My mom is going to let me use her good printer for the poster. It can print on larger paper and the resolution is outstanding."

"That'll make things easier," said Justin. "Look what we found. It's perfect." He moved back so Eddy could see the image of an eddy coil used in a recycling plant. Eddy agreed that it was just what the poster needed and loaded the image onto his flash drive along with the eddy coil diagram from the old poster.

"Come on." Eddy led Justin and Terry into his mom's usually off-limits studio, which was really just a room with a computer and a table and a futon couch. The studio became a guest room when they had company. The room was tidier than Eddy remembered ever seeing it. He printed the images, and they arranged them on the living room floor.

The process continued as Eddy wound the coil, dictating to Justin, who typed in the text describing how an eddy coil works, how it is used in a recycling plant, and how it might (someday, theoretically, emphasized Eddy) be used to propel objects in space. Justin offered suggestions to make Eddy's explanations clearer to people who did not already know all about electromagnetism. Eddy occasionally put down the coil for a trip to the printer.

Terry worked on the poster layout, including a drawing of a (fictional) mass driver launching a payload from the surface of the Moon. She had found that image on one of her favorite fiction science sites.

Fact Number 300 from the Random Access Memory of Edison Thomas: Mass Driver 1, the first prototype mass driver, was built by students at the Massachusetts Institute of Technology in 1976 and 1977, under the direction of Gerard K. O'Neill and Henry Kolm.

—

Aside from a short break for dinner of roast chicken (*Gallus domesticus*), corn (*Zea mays*), and mashed potatoes (*Solanum tuberosum*), work continued into the evening. Eddy finished winding the coil just as Terry put some finishing touches on the poster, using blue and green markers to make a decorative border. Eddy, Justin, and Terry stood around the poster, admiring the product of their teamwork.

Terry looked at her watch. "Oh no, I promised my mom I'd be home by 8:00."

"I gotta go, too," said Justin. "See you tomorrow." He grabbed his bike helmet and jacket next to the front door.

"Yeah, good luck," said Terry. "And get some sleep."

"Thank you," said Eddy. He closed the door behind them and stood looking at the door for a second, then turned to look at the poster on the living room floor. It had turned out better than anything he could have done himself, even if he had had a week to do it. He looked at the repaired coil on the couch and decided that he had time to improve the coil, too. He picked it up and took it to the basement, where he fabricated rings of nickel, aluminum, and steel to add to the copper ring he had used in the demonstration at the Drayton fair.

Eddy didn't go to bed until well past midnight. Even then, he did not sleep well. He spent much of the night composing and practicing the new talk he would give for the judges. This time he would talk about the practical applications of eddy coils, in the present and in the future.

Despite his lack of sleep, he was alert and confident in the morning. Much different from the mornings after his Jim nightmares. And his pillow was dry.

After breakfast (cornflakes, milk, a banana, and OJ), he loaded the coil, metal rings, and transformer into a fresh box and carefully rolled up the poster. The chance of rain was only 10 percent, but he placed the rolled-up poster in a garbage bag to protect it, just in case.

As he loaded the box and poster into the truck, he nearly dropped them when Dad's hand tousled his hair. "Good job, kiddo. The poster is much better than the last one."

"I had some help," admitted Eddy.

"Who from?"

"Just a couple of friends."

"Friends?"

"Yes. I have friends."

"Really? By the way, I got a bill from the city in the mail yesterday. Do you know anything about a stop sign?"

Eddy grimaced, then explained about the traffic device.

"I guess you meant well," said Dad.

"Then I am off the fishhook?"

"I don't know about a 'fishhook,' but you still have to pay for the new sign, if that's what you mean."

"I understand." Maybe Dad hadn't figured out that Eddy had borrowed his good drill bit to use on the stop sign.

"And next time, put my drill bit back where it belongs." Maybe he had.

"Eddy!"

Eddy turned to see Kip walking briskly toward him, waving something over his head.

"I'm glad I caught you," said Kip. "I have something for you." Kip placed a box in Eddy's hands.

"What is it?"

"They're special musician's earplugs. I thought they might come in handy at the science fair. They aren't the expensive custom-fit jobs, but they work pretty well for me. They let you hear what you need to hear, but just makes everything quieter. See, there's a little filter in there."

Eddy turned the clear plastic box over in his hands. The cobalt blue earplugs tumbled, revealing cylindrical inserts. Those must be the low-frequency filters. Eddy had tried using normal earplugs, but they selectively filter out the high frequencies, leaving the annoying rumbles of low frequencies and making everything muffled and distorted, like trying to hear a conversation in the next room.

"Thank you."

It was nearly time to go. Dad had already started the truck.

"No problem. Well, good luck, Eddy," said Kip.

Eddy looked around to make sure Dad couldn't hear and whispered to Kip, "You can call me Edison, but not in front of my dad."

"OK," Kip whispered back. "But don't call me Howard, whatever you do."

"It is a deal."

Eddy jumped as Dad yelled, "Eddy, get in. We need to get going."

Eddy opened the passenger-side door.

"I hope you win," said Kip.

Eddy sat down, closed the door, and buckled his seat belt.

As far as Eddy was concerned, he had already won.

Appendix: Not-So-Random Numbers

0.08 % = legal driving limit for blood alcohol content in most states

1.7 kg = average weight of an adult male duck-billed platypus

2 years = time it takes for a coco de mer nut to germinate

3.1459 = pi, the ratio of the circumference to the diameter of a circle

4.6 = maximum pickle pH

9.80665 m/s² = standard acceleration due to gravity on Earth

20 Hz = lower limit of human hearing

24 = number of chicken eggs required to equal the volume of a single ostrich egg

28 bpm = lowest recorded resting heart rate (Miguel Indurain, five-time winner of the Tour de France bicycle race)

32 = number of permanent teeth in an adult human

44 pounds = weight of the largest lobster on record

73 atm = minimum supercritical pressure of carbon dioxide (above 31.1°C)

75 = number of countries where traffic keeps to the right (compared to 164 countries where traffic keeps to the left)

144 feet = height of tallest known white oak tree

212°F = the boiling point of water

220°F = jellying point at sea level

264 hours = length of voluntary sleep deprivation endured by Randy Gardner in 1964

300 m/s² = acceleration achieved by Mass Driver 1

305 mm = number of mm in a foot

343 m/s = speed of sound in dry air at sea level at 20°C

350 tons = payload of the Terex Titan

475 nm = wavelength of blue light

568 kJ = heat released by the ignition of gunpowder

695 = number of people killed in Missouri, Illinois, and Indiana by the Tri-State Tornado on March 18, 1925.

700 pounds = amount of paper used in a year by the average American

1893 = year in which the U.S. Supreme Court ruled that tomatoes are vegetables, and not fruits (despite the fact that they are botanically classified as fruits).

2,400 = number of soldiers who crossed the Delaware River with George Washington on the night of December 25, 1776.

5,280 feet = number of feet in a mile

17,468 = number of vacuum tubes in the ENIAC

211,646 = number of children under 19 treated for trampoline injuries in 2003

1,500,000 volts = electrical current generated by the Mid-America Science Museum Tesla coil

4,800,000 years = time since the Pliocene Epoch, when woolly mammoths first appeared

299,792,458 m/s = speed of light

600,000,000 = peak population of rabbits in Australia in the 1950s

5,000,000,000 = estimated number of passenger pigeons in North America at the beginning of European colonization

9,192,631,770 Hz = frequency of vibration of a cesium-133 atom

10^{100} = 1 googol, the number after which the search engine Google was named